SOMETHING BLACK IN
THE LENTIL SOUP

SOMETHING BLACK IN THE LENTIL SOUP

Reshma S. Ruia

BLACKAMBER BOOKS

Published in 2003 by
BlackAmber Books
3 Queen Square
London WC1N 3AU

1 3 5 7 9 10 8 6 4 2

A full CIP record for this book is available from the British Library.

ISBN 1–901969–14–2

Typeset in 12.5/13.5 pt Garamond Three
by RefineCatch Limited, Bungay, Suffolk
Printed and bound in Finland by WS Bookwell

Acknowledgements

~⌒

Many thanks to Rosemarie Hudson for her enthusiasm in seeing this into print, to Lynn Curtis and Helen Simpson for their astute editorial comments and Fiona Oldfield for administrative assistance. Thanks also to Michael Schmidt for his unwavering encouragement. Last but not the least, my gratitude to Raj Ruia for his constant love and support, to Ravi and Sabrina for putting up with a 'writing mum', and to Himani and Preeti for sisterly solidarity.

FOR MY PARENTS

CHAPTER ONE

Before it all began:
Delhi scenes from the Seventies

॰

With a tattered cloud
as my roof,
the broken tip of a sun-beam
as my guiding ray,
I will be like the lotus
that throws away its root
only to touch the skies.

(Lines penned by Naidu at the age of twenty-one)

IF YOU TOOK the second road to the right of Minto Bridge, past the washerwomen's *bustee* and Balwant Rai's teashop, stopping just before the Delhi branch of the Church of Scientology, you would reach our house. The household, consisting of my parents, my wife Kamala and Feroze, my son, occupied the ground floor of number twenty-three Rouse Avenue. These were a modest set of flats built for Ministry *babus* with modest official means. It was a colony of bicycles and two-wheeler Vespas and housewives who grumbled over the price of sugar. Only Mr Basu, our upstairs neighbour,

1

boasted a car, a Fiat Padmini which coughed into life during the Pooja holidays, when Mr Basu visited his relatives in Chitteranjan Park.

The flats overlooked a large, dusty green patch in the middle. It was here that the children and mothers congregated every evening in a burst of noisy play and gossip. This came to an abrupt halt once the washerwomen from across the road claimed the space as their local latrine. Repeated complaints to the Municipal Board fell on deaf ears, and dark rumours about typhoid and cholera began circulating among the mothers. It was only when our neighbour from number twenty-six, a retired Army man who had seen action in Burma, appointed himself upholder of our garden's hygiene that a solution was found. Every sunrise, the upright figure of Colonel Dinshaw would emerge, waving a walking stick, and shoo the women away like a flock of frightened crows, just as they were about to squat, saris lifted in an untidy roll round their knees, the little tin of water within hand's reach.

Built during the giddy Socialist flutter of the Sixties, the Rouse Avenue flats were a sad reminder of romance gone sour. The magnolia-cream paint imported so lovingly from Tashkent had become, by 1972, an untidy wash of sickly yellow, and every monsoon Kamala would rush about the rooms placing buckets at strategic points to collect the leaking overflow from the Polish drain pipes. Yet this general shabbiness lay hidden beneath a picturesque riot of bougainvillaea which bloomed, rain or drought, bleeding colour into every nook and cranny in the walls, so that the flats, when viewed from a distance, seemed to be floating in a basket of flowers.

Amma stubbornly hung on to the government flat even after Father passed away with sudden chest pains while queuing patiently at the Mother Dairy milk depot for his daily glass of unadulterated buffalo milk. It was Mrs Basu, our ever-present, ever-helpful neighbour from upstairs, who came running to inform us of his collapse, her still-wet hair spread like a limp, open fan upon plump hunched shoulders. *'Hai Ram, Bap re Bap.'* Mrs Basu's tongue tripped over the Hindi vowels in excitement. She had been drying her hair on the terrace when the commotion around the milk depot attracted her eye and ear.

How well I remember that moment. I was just setting off for the Ministry of Education, where I held the socially sensitive job of monitoring the scholarship needs of the minority communities in government schools. Kamala was busy forcing the last bite of *alu paratha* into Feroze's reluctant mouth while he stood fidgeting with his school bag, and Amma as usual sat on the veranda, fiddling with the knobs on her Murphy radio, trying to catch the BBC World Service.

Mrs Basu's news fell like a thunderbolt. Feroze collapsed on the veranda floor, tears streaming down his cheeks. Kamala immediately slammed shut all the windows and wordlessly handed Amma a plain cream sari from the bottom of her Godrej almirah. Contrary to all expectations, I, Kavi Naidu, took the news like a man. The moment, as I explained in a subsequent poem, marked a watershed, a transition to the travails of manhood when, like Wordsworth, 'I put away childish things'.

Quietly I shut the bedroom door against the sound of Kamala's noisy weeping. Emerging only at sunset, I

3

silently pressed a poem into Amma's hand, ignoring the bewildered expressions of those around us.

'Shirker. Is that how a son is meant to behave? Not even bothering about the funeral arrangements,' Mrs Basu mumbled as Amma silently clutched the poem to her heart.

'Look at this, *behanji*. Such mature handling of grief. Just listen to his feelings on mortality and death. My Kavi is no shrinking violet:

> 'There is a skull,
> Hiding behind your young child's smile.
> It is not a rattle that he shakes but the
> Bones in his body.'

The poem agitated the usually placid Kamala, who quickly placed a black *tikka* behind Feroze's left ear to ward off the evil eye. My mother, despite the gravity of the moment, appreciated this literary outpouring, and urged me to submit it to the Ministry's annual newsletter: 'Who knows which influential chord it might strike?' It appeared in the Diwali edition of the newsletter and, much to my delight, I found myself somewhat of a celebrity within the typing pool. Even Miss Sinha, Mr Gupta's brown-eyed steno, who always made a point of asking after Feroze, begged for her own personal signed copy.

CHAPTER TWO

From the family album

~

THE NAIDU FAMILY could be described, in all honesty, as one of potential overachievers. There was Mother, or Amma as she was universally known (on account of the South Indian saris she favoured), with her Nehru Appreciation Society (NAPS for short), which she had been running with quiet efficiency for the past dozen years. The highlight was the annual newsletter, with its tit-bits of little-known facts about the great leader's life, which went out to the subscribers scattered around the country.

Amma's passion for Nehru was strictly apolitical. It was the turn of his cheekbone, his command of English grammar, the graceful, almost feminine way in which he carried himself, that she admired, qualities which in her opinion were sadly lacking in modern India and therefore worthy of national dissemination. Every November (the fourteenth being Nehruji's birthday), a Nehru lookalike contest was held and the general public encouraged to send in candidates' photographs. The winner for the past five years had been the same retired wrestler from Hyderabad with sensitive drooping eyes, who had accumulated in the process five copies of

Glimpses of World History, and five handwritten congratulatory letters from Amma.

While he was with us, Father indulged this schoolgirl passion with an amused, almost proud, sense of proprietorship. 'A flowering of her intellect, this is what your mother is going through,' he said the day NAPS was established as a non-profit-making charitable institution under Section 3.4 AE of the Indian Private Societies Act. In Father's eyes this raised her above the general cut and thrust of Indian womanhood in the neighbourhood, the sort who preened about knitting their own mufflers and grinding their own garam masala. He even allowed me, his only son, to be named Jawahar, though after the publication of my first poem in the *Illustrated Weekly Views* I chose to abandon this in favour of the more poetic Kavi. It was only my maternal grandmother, living in the sleepy town of Kanpur, who persisted in addressing me as Jawahar.

After Father's passing away our household routine quietly re-established itself. Amma threw herself with renewed zeal into her Nehru Society. She still defiantly wore her colourful-bordered silks and listened to the BBC World Service, and her only concession to widowhood was a sudden aversion to buffalo's milk. In a surprising twist of Gandhian austerity, she voiced a stubborn craving for goat's milk. Diligent enquiries eventually led me to the Hindu Abandoned Animal Centre (HAAC) in old Delhi, run by a politician's wife as a vote-attracting gimmick. It then fell upon Kamala as the dutiful daughter-in-law to ensure that the amiable female goat I procured was fed and milked each morning, and the milk taken, froth still lining the edge of the steaming tumbler, to Amma's room.

My poetic muse could only blossom in such a rarefied domestic atmosphere. That this muse took the linguistic form of English seemed natural. Being a loyal devotee of Nehruji, Amma insisted that we even dreamed in English. Every significant Saturday of my boyhood was taken up queuing patiently with Father for the twenty-five-minute bus ride to the British Council, where the morning was spent browsing through leather-bound editions of Charles Dickens and Sir Walter Scott. I was sure our familiar figures provided an endless source of comfort to the lonely-looking Anglo-Indian ladies who religiously patrolled the shelves. Much to our disappointment, they politely rebuffed all attempts at friendship, despite years of regular visits. Any query regarding a third renewal of *Ivanhoe* or the waiving of a fine was always met by the same tight-lipped shake of the head and a quick smoothing of the ruffled blouse that they all seemed to favour.

'*Bechari*, poor souls, stranded in this hot country with that all-milk complexion and nobody to call their own,' Father would comment, on coming out of the coolness of the air-conditioned building into the blinding heat outside.

Unknown to him, there was someone feverishly plotting urgent schemes to end their loneliness. From the age of thirteen or so, the same dream awkwardly visited me without fail on Saturday nights. A faintly perspiring librarian would approach me with a shy smile and, with trembling hands, hold out the latest leather-bound edition of one of my works. With an equally tender smile, I would sign the book and press it back into her hands. This accidental touching of hands then progressed to a touching of lips and a whispered proposal of marriage.

CHAPTER THREE

I stumble upon a gift

⌇

THE CLARION CALL of poetry did not come until my first year of college at Kishori Mal. Through a cruel accident of fate, my modest final Senior Cambridge marks failed to secure me a place at the leading private college in Delhi. Lacking both financial muscle and official IAS connections to push me in through the back door, I was forced to settle for the third-rate educational standards of a *desi* college, where the lingua franca was streetwise Hindi, the reigning role model a greasy-sideburned Bombay film star, and the standard form of greeting a collective, tribal-sounding '*Yaar*'.

I took great care to highlight my difference from this plebeian crowd, refusing, for instance, to succumb to the prevailing fashion for brightly patterned polyester shirts unbuttoned to the waist and high platform shoes with enormous steel buckles. My preferred mode of attire was the sober navy-blue blazer that Amma had rescued from a Christmas jumble sale at the Irish Embassy.

'Remember, son, a dignified jacket and tie is the hallmark of greatness. Just think of Nehruji, and no need to mix with that *junglee* riff-raff,' she would say while packing my butter and jam sandwiches, for in another ideological move I refused to eat in the college canteen, where the menu never gravitated from its parochial offering of *dahi-vada* and samosas. Much to my delight, the students respected this air of exclusivity and kept their distance, barring one or two unsavoury *goonda* types who insisted on heckling me as a 'crackpot type, *yaar*'.

The discovery of my talent came about quite by accident with the second-semester essay on Shakespearean soliloquies. In a moment of pure perspiration mingled with the necessity of fulfilling the word quota, I had penned a few verses of my own as a suitable conclusion. My creativity caught Dr Anand's sharp, incisive eye and he arranged to see me. He was filling in for Mrs Mehta, our uninspiring English lecturer, who was given to bouts of feverish crocheting in the staffroom every lunchtime. Mrs Mehta was absent with some delicate medical complication of a feminine nature, and Dr Anand, normally head of the chemistry department, had graciously stepped in to fill the vacuum.

Dr Anand was not the average textbook *lassi*-guzzling Sikh. This meant he did not immediately *bhangra* leap out of his chair to greet me, or thump me heartily between the shoulder-blades, or belch in the process of telling private-parts jokes. He was a sensitive, scholarly man with stooping shoulders, a neatly trimmed beard, and a sad-looking beige turban which faithfully sheltered him through sun and rain.

Dr Anand motioned me to sit, and retrieved the essay from beneath the latest copy of Mrs Mehta's Indian *Crochet Weekly*. The cover promised a trip to

Singapore for the fortunate winner of its 'Crochet a Diwali Scene' competition.

'Been writing poetry for long?'

My heart did a quick somersault before settling back into place.

'Yes – I mean, no, sir, though I have grown up in a wordy kind of household.'

Dr Anand cleared his throat in approval and started leafing through the essay. 'I particularly like this line: "There comes a tide in the affairs of men."'

It was vital to stop him before creativity was misattributed and authorship misconstrued.

'Sir, if I may . . .' Reclaiming the essay, I turned rapidly to the last two pages, cleared my throat and in my best BBC voice read out:

> 'To be or not to be, he who would be king says
> But would not a better command be TO LIVE.
> So that every new day one
> Could seize with a joyful smile
> And every nightfall greet with a grateful sigh . . .'

I looked expectantly at Dr Anand, who was fidgeting with a glass paperweight where a butterfly lay trapped. Little blue-black veins criss-crossed the tissue-thin wings, which were slowly crumbling to dust within that airless tomb.

'That butterfly, sir.' I pointed to the paperweight. 'How well it illustrates the human condition – flying today, caught tomorrow, hence the universal relevance of the poem.'

Being a scientific man, Dr Anand appeared a bit startled by this philosophical insight. Tiny drops of perspiration clung stubbornly to the ends of his moustache as the ceiling fan above rippled the papers around us with a gentle, dusty sigh.

At last he spoke. ' "To be or not to be . . ." Strange how we scientists shut out the sound of words and are always busy dissecting their meaning. Listen, Naidu, I have a suggestion. My brother-in-law works in the poetry section of the *Illustrated Weekly Views*. They might be interested in this kind of literary highbrow stuff. If you want, I could put in a word for you?'

My hunch about the fatefulness of that day had been right. Suddenly, without actual serious consideration, a career in the world of literature beckoned. Before long I would be enjoying my own legitimate space upon those British Council shelves. Who would have thought that a diminutive, scientific Sikh would one day be responsible for unleashing my hitherto unrecognised muse upon the world? True, there was a momentary stab of disappointment – this patron was no tweed-suited, pipe-smoking English lord. But then again, did not Amma always say opportunity came in every shape and size? The trick was to seize it before it skulked away.

'I would be deeply grateful, sir, if you could be my patron in the writing of this fresh chapter of my life.' I folded my hands gratefully.

Dr Anand, being a man of honour, kept his word. The very next month I accompanied him to the magazine's offices in Pahar Ganj, an unsavoury part of Delhi I usually avoided. A far cry from Lutyens's city with its wide gulmohur tree-frilled avenues and buildings etched in delicate pink sandstone, this was an unholy hotchpotch of man and animal. Dirt and noise overran everything like a chicken-pox rash. How could a magazine of such high repute originate from such cramped, noisy quarters?

The narrow, chipped flight of stairs splattered in *pan*-spit left us both breathless by the time we reached the fourth floor. Little pools of water of doubtful origin lay like exclamation marks on each step. A sharp smell of urea hung in the air, originating no doubt from the gents' urinal located directly opposite the entrance to the building.

'Delhi is fast becoming another Calcutta, don't you think so, sir?' I observed as Dr Anand rubbed away at his forehead with a large hanky.

'It is this damn population, Naidu, that is what is bringing the country down. Too many mouths and buttocks everywhere.'

Taken aback, I put this militant outburst down to his being a professor type. Politics always excited them.

The optimistically named office (it was really a large room cluttered with Godrej desks and whining table fans) was teeming with many *babu* lookalikes running around with ink-stained fingers, shouting loudly to one another. Dr Anand's brother-in-law, one Mr Dhanwa, greeted us warmly and immediately led us to his glass-walled cubicle, bellowing for the peon, who shuffled into the room bearing cups of tea and Glaxo biscuits.

There was deep family love at work here, I thought, observing the affectionate way in which Dr Anand and his brother-in-law hugged each other. As if on some mutual, prearranged cue, both immediately burst into news and counter-news about the goings-on of their various nephews and nieces, who all seemed to be called either Pinky or Tony. As soon as there was a suitable pause in this family bulletin, I quickly brought out my *Hamlet* poem.

'*Chalta hai*, put it away! No need for any reading,' replied the editor, waving aside my hand, which offered the poem like a bouquet of flowers.

'My *jijaji* has brought you. That is the only golden reference I need.'

Dr Anand looked much gratified by this compliment and modestly lowered his eyes to the floor. Mr Dhanwa's big, booming voice shouted something and the door immediately opened to admit an earnest-looking Madrasi gentleman wearing spotless white Keds.

'Here, Subramaniam, make sure this gets published in the next issue, and just contact Seth, will you, for an opening blurb.' My poem rapidly changed hands and the Subramaniam fellow made a speedy exit from the room.

Big and muscular, with flaring nostrils, Mr Dhanwa did not exactly conform to any preconception of a poetry editor.

'Your future is made, son. I am going to get Seth himself to praise your work. He owes me a favour, anyway. As I told you before, any protégé of my *jijaji* deserves to be introduced by the best hands.' And Mr Dhanwa turned to Dr Anand with a smile bright enough to set fire to a monsoon cloud. Overcome by this display of devotion, Dr Anand impulsively leaned forward and pressed both his hands warmly.

The rest of the meeting passed in animated discussion of the possibility of Mr Dhanwa obtaining an American green card. It seemed an application had been forwarded for a position as a mechanic welder in a place called Pittisberg, and the letter of appointment was expected any day. This intended career move to a manual occupation surprised me.

'Why would anyone wish to leave the world of literature, sir?' I asked, interrupting their talk.

'My dear son, tell me, will this literature-viterature build my house in Jallunder or send my son to medical college? But keep on daydreaming anyway like our Rajesh Khanna . . . After all, you're still a starry-eyed young pup.' Mr Dhanwa patted my head most kindly.

The poem on *Hamlet* appeared in the next issue of the *Weekly*, under the headline 'Emerging Stars in the Literary Sky'. Much to my annoyance there were three other novices sharing the limelight, but I was pleased to note that the foreword had been penned by none other than Seth himself, described in the latest *Who's Who* as the 'grand old man of Indian letters'. Father immediately ordered a dozen copies of the *Weekly* from our local newspaperman and personally delivered them to our various friends and wellwishers. A copy was even hand-carried to the British Council.

Now that the title 'poet' could legitimately be claimed, the business of my being a student seemed futile. That evening I bundled away the syllabus books (barring *Roget's Thesaurus* and *Palgrave's Golden Treasury*) into a dark corner of Amma's almirah. Much to my delight, she wholeheartedly supported this new turn of events. After all, hadn't Nehruji also displayed a literary bent, and who knew what dizzy heights this new vocation would lead to?

'But he still needs to study. After all, we won't be here for ever, you know. We must make sure he settles down, gets a decent job.'

'Tell me, what glory have you found in being a *babu?*' Amma dismissed Father's conventional fears with a contemptuous wave of her hand. 'Your aspirations have always been pea-sized. I have other global plans for our son. Be like a tornado in your ambition, son. Remember, even you are entitled to a "tryst with destiny".'

My hunched figure, steeped in intense thought over an open exercise book, soon became a familiar sight to the retired strollers and the various sweepers and vegetable wallahs who descended upon Rouse Avenue in a flurry of self-important activity each morning.

Mrs Basu from upstairs dropped in from time to time to check on my progress. 'Bringing a little sweetmeat to sweeten the sweat.' With a self-conscious little laugh, she would slowly coax a coconut *burfi* into my mouth. Being a Bengali, reared on the poetry of Tagore and the novels of Sarat Chandra Bose, she fully sympathised with my new calling.

'Don't listen to them, *behanji*,' she reassured Amma, after a stream of panic-stricken letters written by Naniji arrived from Kanpur, demanding to know whether it was true that Jawahar, her only grandson, had grown his hair long and become a *devdas* or loafer. 'Do you want your only son to be a rat, stuck in this rat-racing world competition?'

Father, however, was not entirely convinced of the sincerity behind these stirring words of Mrs Basu. And rightly so, for soon afterwards we learned that her own son, a roguish-looking boy called Chintu, had successfully made it through the second round of the Indian Civil Service exams. 'The king of all rat-racing competitions!' Mr Basu jubilantly informed us, and

15

Mrs Basu herself was seen triumphantly distributing boxes of Haldi Ram sweets to all the neighbours.

In the months that followed I usually penned a poem before leaving reluctantly for college. (Father insisted that I sit through a minimum number of lectures to earn a degree of some class.) Mother would then quickly check it for grammatical errors, make a cyclostyled copy and file it carefully under an alphabetical theme listing. Father even took some poems to Balwant Rai's teashop-cum-STD-booth round the corner and pestered him into pinning the Hindi translation just behind the counter where the rusks and the Parle biscuits were kept.

For some inexplicable reason, it was women's magazines, especially those from the south, who most readily recognised the poignancy of my verse. In fact, the editor of one Malyalam ladies' weekly even requested a reprint of the *Hamlet* poem in two successive issues. I had less luck with the more heavyweight journals like the *Modern Literary Review.* Repeated submissions were simply returned unopened.

'Connections, that's what's needed in such places. How I wish your father knew someone in the publishing world. But no need to worry, there will be all-round regrets once your star has risen, son.' Amma reinforced each encouraging word with a jab of her knife as she set about peeling the potatoes for dinner that night.

CHAPTER FOUR

A friendship is struck

⌒

IT WAS DURING one of the temporary lulls in the publication of my poems that the decision to cultivate the society of like-minded souls came about.

'There is no point in you slogging away all alone; one needs cross-pollination of ideas in order to grow. You must make friends. Discuss. Argue.' This was Father at his earnest best on a Sunday morning, replete with cups of ginger tea, *gobi parathas* and the second-hand wisdom of weekend papers.

Amma, on the other hand, vigorously opposed any form of interaction. 'What pollination? More like pollution, if you ask me. All this talk-valk will just taint the purity of your poems.'

Every poet worth his verse used to hang around Todar Mal Road in those heady days of the early Seventies. The 'arty-farty mile', as the locals called it, stretched from Billo Ram's *chaat* house at one end to the Sapru Centre, headquarters of All-India Radio, at the other. In between lay the Triveni Theatre with its open-air auditorium, the Natural Science Museum with its distinctive sundial from the Maurya period, and the American Cultural Center, which was shortly relocating to a leafier South Delhi suburb.

17

Squeezed self-consciously between these imposing buildings was Billo's *chaat* house, which specialised in authentic Bombay *bhel* and was a particular favourite with the militant sort of female student, a type I carefully avoided in college, a type who insisted on wearing large ten-paisa-sized *bindis* on their foreheads and dressed their arms in a noisy confusion of oxidised silver bangles. This artistic oasis became my haunt. I would skip the afternoon lectures, buy the evening edition of the *Patriot*, a left-wing journal favoured by the intelligentsia, and establish myself at Billo's, hoping to strike some publisher's eye, for the café served as an informal club for the tried and tested thinkers of Delhi.

Billo's could not strictly be defined as an intellectual's hangout. For one thing, it lacked the air of gloom and suppressed passion that usually typifies such places, at least in the Russian novels I had started reading of late. This was a large, air-conditioned place with marble-topped tables and a cut-glass chandelier imported all the way from Dubai. Bright tubular lights encircled the walls like lurid neon-coloured snakes, and dominating the cash-till located near the entrance was a larger-than-life picture of Hanumanji, embroidered, it was rumoured, with real Benarasi gold thread.

Malicious whispers circulated about the source of Billo's wealth. It seemed money had been made smuggling Johnny Walker from Nepal, and the Senior Commissioner in the Revenue Department himself enjoyed a large slice of the action. I firmly refused to believe such stories, for there couldn't be a humbler man than Billo Ram. Small and rotund, like a pure ghee *laddu*, with hands constantly folded, Billo made a point of personally welcoming each customer with a heartfelt greeting. I found this quite moving and, despite my dislike of the inartistic decor, continued frequenting the place, where my staple order of cucumber and chutney sandwiches, with an extra helping of onions, was always followed by a double mango milkshake.

My regular appearance and slight air of preoccupied creativity as I scribbled a line had the desired effect. One day Sharmila Sharma, a promising playwright whose Marathi adaptation of *The Plague* had recently been staged at Triveni, came over to my table.

'Look here,' she said, without any formal introduction, 'stop this gawking from a distance. We' – she pointed to her friends, who monopolised the same table every day – 'have decided to be nice to you. Especially if you turn out to be a rich *bania*. Anyway, how about treating everybody to a cup of *chai*?'

I could not sleep that night from excitement. I was about to recreate an Oxford don's study, a Left Bank café, right in the heart of Billo's *chaat* house.

Sharmila's friends were a colourful, untidy group. I would normally have thought twice about associating with them, but the pursuit of artistic dialogue made it a necessity. Often, on my return from the *chaat*-house discussions, Amma pressed me about the peculiarities of my new-found friends, and I would give carefully edited descriptions of Romesh or Binoy or Urvashi. For instance, Binoy wore his hair in a ponytail, and Romesh, I was sure, smoked an undesirable sort of cigarette. The biggest revelation was Urvashi, who had left her husband and five-year-old son and now openly cohabited with another woman.

19

In some respects, I thought, as yet another discussion ended in a barrage of oaths and abuse, my new friends were but a refined version of the Kishori Mal students. True, they all spoke English beautifully, but the talk invariably wound itself around sexual escapades and vicious backstabbing of mutual acquaintances. Fiercely possessive of their creativity, they stubbornly refused to share with me the fruits of their ongoing labour.

'Just drop the idea, *yaar*. What guarantee is there that you won't steal away my twenty-four-carat gem? This is India, after all. No bloody copyright, just bloody copycat,' Binoy said, insolently blowing little smoke-rings into my face.

But what hurt most was their complete lack of interest in my work. I had, for instance, once shown Sharmila a poem in progress. She looked at it carelessly and then immediately launched into a description of her Marathi translation of an Ibsen play.

Seth. He was the barometer the group used to gauge every achievement and failure. But when I asked which aspect of his verse they most admired, Romesh broke into a coarse laugh.

'It is not the verse we are talking about, damn it! It's his bloody virility. That man carries magnet balls in his VIP underwear.'

Even the girls giggled, and Sharmila brazenly boasted, 'Tell me about it. I tell you that man's battery is ever ready.'

Fresh tea and *lassi* were ordered and the talk went back to Urvashi's curious preference for Nepalese girls, Urvashi happening to be away that day.

My new friends were very – I had found the term just recently – 'avant-garde'.

20

'They are ahead of our times, Amma. In fact, they consider me rather old-fashioned.' There was hurt in my voice as I said this, for I had just learned that a New Year's holiday to Goa had been arranged behind my back. The youth hostel was booked and Urvashi and Sharmila were excitedly planning to be India's first female streakers.

'What old-fashioned? They are just plain old jealous of your smartness. How I wish you mingled with more Oxford types,' Amma replied, running fond fingers through my thick, wavy hair.

CHAPTER FIVE

An accidental encounter

〰

MY FIRST MEETING with Seth took place in less than
auspicious circumstances. It happened when Sharmila
Sharma, in a rare show of artistic camaraderie, lent me
the script of her forthcoming play about the impact of
the Mughal invasion on the modern female Indian
psyche. While promising to be as critically helpful as I
could (I had great faith in Sharmila's intellectual prowess), I was puzzled by certain stylistic shortcomings.
Phrases such as 'And they lay side by side, indifferent,
like two slabs of meat on ice', with their cold,
functional imagery, were tasteless, to say the least.

It was to illustrate the dignity of English prose that I
made my way to Sharmila's *barsati* that August day.
She lived on the top floor of one of those huge Satyajit
Ray-style crumbling mansions converted into over-
crowded flats which were rapidly fading through
benign governmental indifference. The marble stucco
front lay hidden behind a criss-cross of washing lines
and stranded pigeon nests. A huge peepul tree, all
twisted trunk and knotted roots, rose painfully through
the earth. By its side lay a broken fountain. Tall,
menacing-looking Greek goddesses sprouted from its

cracked mouth. I took great care to observe these details, having recently read in a reputed British journal about the importance of introducing topographical detail in one's poetry.

I admired Sharmila's bravery in choosing to live alone in such hardship, purely in pursuit of the artistic vision. But how could her parents be so careless about letting loose a young girl in a city as wild and modern as Delhi? A flamboyant OM sign drawn in red *sindoor* greeted me when I finally reached the right door. The long tentacles of a luxuriant money plant almost hiding the doorbell reminded me of Sharmila's long, thick plaits, which often brushed against my face when she leaned forward to stress a point.

The door gave way to my gentle push. What struck me immediately was the violence of the colours on the walls. Peacock blues and lotus pinks fought with sunny yellows and oranges. Mirrored hangings from Rajasthan took pride of place, and reflected in each of their winking mirrors was the image of a man seated on a low divan, fondling a single upturned breast. The breast, I found, lowering my gaze to the divan, belonged to none other than my friend Sharmila Sharma.

There she lay, eyes shut, head cradled in a middle-aged lap (the man was definitely forty-plus, judging by the grey in his hair). The stone-coloured buttons of her crumpled shirt were open. From it rose that shell-smooth curve, one brown nipple defiantly brushing against the long, lean fingers of the unknown man. It was my first encounter with three-dimensional sex, and which way could I look?

The man spoke first, staring through me into the open doorway, one hand still absent-mindedly playing with the exposed flesh. He had a low, deep voice, and spoke in what years of exposure to the BBC World Service had trained me to recognise as a pure Oxford accent.

'You have a visitor, Sharmila. Better pack up the meat.' The hands expertly bundled back her nakedness into the shirt.

'Kavi! Shit! You? So typical. Bringing back the script in person.' Sharmila sprang up from the divan, giving a most unfeminine undisguised yawn. 'I suppose, now that you're here, I ought to play hostess.'

I was expecting tears of shame, pleas for forgiveness, some explanation about a yogic massage, not this cool-as-a-cucumber greeting.

'You'll have *jal jeera*, won't you? Madness to have tea in this heat,' Sharmila's irritated voice called from behind the sari partition that hid the kitchen.

I drank the sour coldness greedily, and immediately felt better. After all, Sharmila was hardly a sister or a daughter; her private morals were her own private business.

The middle-aged man made no attempt to re-enter the conversation. He had thrown himself against the cushions and was leafing through some foreign magazine in a bored sort of way. That he was handsome there could be no denying. Even I, a man, could appreciate that. With that aquiline nose and fair skin, he could almost pass for an Englishman. This was obviously what Amma meant when she went on about Nehruji's petal-pink complexion.

'I am Kavi Naidu, sir, a poet and an old friend of Sharmila's.' Hand outstretched, I approached the seated man, whose identity I was determined to uncover.

'A poet? Hmmm, indeed? And where have you suddenly sprung from?' An all-appraising stare drilled holes through me. 'Anyway, since you insist on describing yourself as a poet, the reading we're holding next week at the Fine Arts Auditorium should be of interest. You might pick up some useful tips.' He gazed at me unblinkingly, clearly not expecting a response. 'Well, Sharmila, I must be off now – another tedious cocktail party at the Belgian Embassy.'

And he was gone, but not before biting Sharmila's lips in a full-frontal kiss. I had never seen Indians kiss before, believing it to be a Western custom. The naked brutality of the act left me quite breathless.

The door shut and Sharmila turned to me with a wide-eyed smile. 'You lucky bastard! You've been invited to a poetry reading by none other than Seth Sahib himself.'

'Seth? Was that really him? You mean, the one you all go so gaga about? The Asian Shakespeare? I didn't know you were related.' Vague titbits of information filtered back into my mind. Didn't that piece in *Who's Who* say there was a wife who was a Professor of Sociology at JNU and two teenaged sons doing business studies in America? But Sharmila wasn't a sociologist, and surely she was too young to be his wife?

'Married to Seth? Don't be so bloody dumb, Naidu. As though I want to be tied down like that at my age.'

And taking a *bidi* from the bookshelf, Sharmila settled back to read through the script, one hand absent-mindedly scratching the inside of her thigh.

CHAPTER SIX

The company of poets

~

IN THE END, it was Amma not Sharmila who accompanied me to the poetry recital at AIFACS Hall. Sharmila went down with hepatitis B and lost no time in catching the next train home to her parents' house in Poona.

A huge *papier-mâché* statue of Ganesha suddenly erupted into light on the stage as a young girl started on a long, intricate Bharat Natyam routine. Restless, and keen to see my fellow poets — or fellow soul-sufferers, as I liked to describe them to Mrs Basu — I decided on impulse to go backstage and introduce myself. Amma thought rapidly for a moment and then, opening her purse, pressed into my hand the rubber-band-tied bundle of what I considered to be my best poems.

A bitter-smelling smoke floated through the back room like an oversized cloud. The outlines gradually emerged of a dozen or so male shapes lolling about on the carpet, heavily engrossed in a game of cards. Several darkish bottles, definitely not Thumbs Up, stood huddled together in the centre.

I spotted Seth immediately. How could he be missed when he sat erect, wearing a paper-crisp Lucknavi *kurta* decorated with a single rose? Maybe it was a trick of the light or the smoke, but I thought everybody else looked smaller and darker in comparison.

Seth looked up without interest while a voice shouted, 'Come on, *yaar*, join us. I bet you play rummy like a bitch!'

I folded my hands in greeting and found a clean spot on the carpet to sit. Questioning glances and raised eyebrows surrounded me. Seth, busy lighting his cigarette, made no attempt at introductions.

I said, 'Let me begin by saying how deeply I admire your works.' Only appreciation, as my friend Sharmila constantly reminded me, would secure entry into this world. How I hoped they could not detect the ignorance lurking behind those words, for I religiously restricted myself to Anglo-Saxon writings.

'Something fishy-fishy, *yaar*. What are you after? Look, we have no jobs or women to hand out,' a coarse voice, definitely a Jat's, slurred from somewhere at the back. A chorus of giggles received this.

'Please.' I folded my hands again. 'Please don't insult the honour of your craft.' Silently I searched for the most eloquent phrase. 'I have, by the grace of God, been granted the gift of poetry, as Seth Sahib himself will attest. I only wish to be recognised as one of you.'

Seth listened with an amused smile and, turning to me, began to explain in a patient, long-suffering voice. 'You poor thing, so desperate to become a part of this literati-glitterati world. Let me put you out of your misery by explaining how this whole scenario really works. Listen.'

He raised his hand and the voices in the room died down obediently.

27

'Once that spotty, flat-chested girl finishes her classical somersaulting on the stage' – a loud laugh greeted this description – 'and the audience has clapped itself silly, the organiser, some bespectacled Madrasi virgin who has been wetting her petticoat for the past six months in fear of this moment, will in a trembling voice ask the Chief Minister to bless the occasion. That constipated fool, being a VIP, will naturally be late. Probably busy humping his mistress at the nearest five-star hotel.'

Seth paused and looked around to gauge the response.

'Hmmm, where was I, now? I hope you're taking notes, Naidu. That's the name, isn't it?' I nodded silently.

'Come on, Seth Sahib, don't stop. You're doing a bloody great job.' It was the Sher-e-Kashmir again, now fondling a bottle between his legs. A burst of applause reinforced his words, and Seth looked at me triumphantly.

I felt humbled. Only the bitterness of a tortured soul could force Seth to speak like this. He must have seen, have felt, so much, even though his lavatorial description of humanity would perhaps have been better softened.

'Please, sir, I only wish to be introduced as a newcomer. Here, take these, my humble first offering.'

And most sincerely I pressed my poems into Seth's hands, which were again expertly dealing the cards.

'The poor bastard! Seth Sahib, put the *chamcha* out of his misery, read his bloody poems, tell him he's a goddamn Ghalib, the new Tagore!' an impatient, drunken voice cried.

'Please, sir, my mother is sitting in the audience. She would be so proud if you could just mention me, or perhaps I could read a short poem of mine? My bio-data is at the back, maybe the *Hamlet* poem. I am in the fifth row. I can quickly come up to the stage.' I pressed Seth's hand eagerly as the door opened and a slim Madrasi lady wearing thick glasses entered the room.

'Please, gentlemen. The Chief Minister has arrived. We will be starting shortly.'

The rest of the evening was a blur. I sat next to Amma, tense with nervous excitement. The poets came and went but I did not pay much attention, so intent was I on catching the sound of my name. Seth, the star of the evening, finally took the microphone and in a detached voice read excerpts from his forthcoming book, a collaboration with a South American poet. The audience rose spontaneously to their feet as the Madrasi lady came forward and, with shaking hands, put a sandalwood garland round Seth's neck. By popular demand, he was requested to recite his most famous poem, the one that had made him a household name at twenty.

'I will leave a map of angry nails upon your skin.
Lay a spit of curses at your door . . .
I will summon the jackals to howl in your blood.
Command the sun to wipe itself blank.
And all because you chose to turn your face
Away from me that summer's day.'

Appreciative cries of 'Wah, wah . . . Bravo' ran through the audience and Seth bowed in a reluctant way. I weakly joined in the clapping, even though I found the imagery far too unrefined and violent for my taste.

It was almost dawn by the time the *mushaira* finished and Amma, concerned by the tiredness on my face, decided to take a taxi home. The taxi rank was a good ten-minute walk and we had to shake a sleepy *sardarji* out of his charpoy.

'You stay in bed late tomorrow. No writing. Tired minds can't create,' Amma admonished me as we patiently waited for the *sardarji* to finish tying up his turban.

Suddenly a fleet of white official-looking Ambassadors sped by, sirens cutting through the ribbon of early-morning stillness. Sitting in one of them was Seth, laughing appreciatively at something the Chief Minister had just said.

I was not to meet Seth directly again until we were both united in London by an inexplicable twist of fate as fellow competitors for the Commonwealth Poetry Prize.

CHAPTER SEVEN

A question of dal and roti

⤛

DESPITE MY LOWER-SECOND-CLASS degree, Lady Luck remained kind, for soon afterwards Father ran into an old classmate of his, a Mr Gupta, at Krishna Opticians in Lajpat Nagar. Once fond reminiscences had been exchanged about their *gulli-danda* days at the Rohtak government school, and the reputations of old school friends satisfactorily butchered and laid to rest, Father invited him and his wife to dinner.

This impromptu invitation required certain alterations to our usual household arrangements. For instance, Amma took the liberty of borrowing Mrs Basu's imported polyester tablecloth. The Basus took merciless advantage of this impending dinner party to emphasise the financial gulf between our two families. Mrs Basu offered to lend Amma her Japanese oven; that is, if she wished to make a baked dish for her guests.

'But why should I be baking a cake for them, Mrs Basu?' Amma used the formal title as a rebuke.

'You don't know these government wives, *behanji*,' Mrs Basu insisted. 'They are very modern and most up-to-date in their cooking tastes.' But Amma refused to budge, and the offer of the oven was withdrawn in a huff.

Mr Basu was keen to learn the identity of the guests, questioning Father in a friendly, persistent way on their early morning walks. On learning that Mr Gupta was a Section One officer in the Education Ministry, with ten remaining years of service, he quietly disclosed his ownership of a red-label bottle of Scotch.

'I know this officer type. They want their daily peg and my bottle is genuine foreign stuff. Guaranteed to make a good impression. And after a peg or two, who knows what favours may fall in your lap?'

But Father refused to budge from his teetotaller principles. Two bottles of soda from Shanker Market were to be the only concession to intoxicants in the house.

The house felt almost festive as preparations for the dinner commenced. Freshly cut chicken was bought from the Muslim butcher at Shanker Market and, finding a Scottish recipe in an old issue of *Good House-keeping*, Amma decided on an adventurous concoction including raisins and cider. Father, meanwhile, learned from an inside source that Mrs Gupta had a fondness for fish. The chicken was hastily discarded and, rather reluctantly, Amma agreed to accept Mrs Basu's offer to cook fried pomfret with mustard seed and crushed red chilli paste.

'I am telling you, she will be licking her fingers clean. We Bengalis, we know how to fry the soul of a fish.' I always admired Mrs Basu's eloquent delivery.

The feast did not go unrewarded. Once the third helping of pomfret had been washed down with liberal lashings of soda, a general feeling of well-being came over the Guptas. Mrs Gupta, a small, quiet woman, seemed genuinely moved by my poetry, which Amma had taken the liberty of reciting. She whispered something long and extended into her husband's ear.

'*Behanji.*' Abruptly Mr Gupta leaned towards Amma, upsetting the little containers of rice pudding on the table. '*Behanji*, I have decided to help your son. There happens to be a vacant post for a Lower Divisional Clerk in my division. Technically it is reserved for the scheduled castes, but I have some pull in the matter and could bring him in on probation.'

Father folded his hands gratefully, while Amma tried her level best to appear pleased. I knew she considered this a wasteful detour from my true calling.

*

A small plywood-partitioned room right next to the water-cooler was the starting point of my bureaucratic career as an LDC. The room also served as a type of temporary archive. Every two weeks or so the peon Babu Ram would enter with another stack of files, and in a flurry of dust and old Raj Kumar songs muttered under his breath rearrange the files, the new ones being swallowed up and acquiring the same patina of dust and age in no time.

My job was essentially to sift through the scholarship requests for higher education from disadvantaged communities, which included scheduled castes and members of minority religions. Being a protégé of Mr Gupta gave me a certain aura of importance, and whispers ran round that I was a mole planted there to report on lapses in punctuality. That my connection with Mr Gupta was but tenuous, however, soon became apparent when he made no attempt to introduce me to his superiors or to invite me for lunch in the senior staff canteen. As per Amma's instructions, I had initially tried hard to strike up a familiar camaraderie, addressing him as 'Uncleji' and dropping into his room without a prior appointment. But Mr Gupta soon put a stop to that.

'Look, Naidu,' he said, while Miss Sinha, the typist, sat waiting, brown eyes demurely lowered, pen poised over a shorthand pad. 'Nothing of this Uncle-Vuncle business any more. I will be "Sir" from now on. And no rushing into the room without permission. Confidential points of national importance are being almost always discussed.' He paused and wiped his glasses.

My eyes filled with tears at the unexpected rebuke. That was the trouble with being artistic: one's feelings always threatened to overflow.

Mysteriously, this conversational exchange soon filtered through the corridors and I began to detect a certain carelessness in the behaviour of those around me. Babu Ram the peon, for instance, stopped bringing me my early-morning tea, and one day I overheard him say, 'Why, he is a nobody really, just stuck his foot into the back door and got in, and there is my nephew sitting unemployed at home with a double doctorate in history and . . .'

In a replay of my Kishori Mal days, I decided to distance myself from this intrigue-ridden mob and concentrate instead on doing the minimum required to hold on to the job with dignity, while maintaining a pleasant but distant demeanour.

Mr Gupta's behaviour puzzled me no end. The generous uncle who had sucked so appreciatively at the pomfret bones had been replaced by someone who passed me unsmilingly in the corridors or scowled critically as I punctually left for home at quarter to five.

CHAPTER EIGHT

Matrimonial pursuits

〜

A STEADY JOB, and for the government at that, could lead to but one thing: matrimony. Aunts with marriageable daughters started making unnaturally attentive enquiries about my well-being, and Amma was at the receiving end of several unexpected lunch invitations. To be perfectly honest, this sudden interest was secretly to my liking. After all, didn't most of my poems have pining for love as their central theme? I had definite ideas about my matrimonial muse. She would be fair-skinned with waist-length hair, convent-educated and modest in demeanour, appreciative of English poetry, and, above all, completely devoted to Amma.

It was the physical practicalities involved in uniting with such a woman that bothered me. My carnal acquaintance with women to date was largely theoretical, the incident with Sharmila Sharma being the only first-hand source of knowledge. True, there had been a few hello-bye-type relationships with girls at Kishori Mal College, but I simply could not equate their nervous giggles and library talk with the existence of breasts and hips. Being an only child with no close youthful female relatives at hand, the unveiling of the female form remained but a vague idea, substantiated only when I was forced to look discreetly through the German magazines smuggled in by Chintu, Mrs Basu's sneaky son.

He perversely timed his visits for when I was at my most vulnerable, various bodily parts on fire and with hands which didn't know which way to wander. This typically occurred during the hot, heavy monsoon afternoons of the summer holidays, when the women of the locality were asleep under furiously humming fans, their starched cotton saris spread stiffly around them like many-petalled flowers, the slow stain of sweat on their blouses steadily drying to a trickle.

I would be in my room playing Snakes and Ladders, fiddling with my shirt buttons or tapping a foot in boredom, when, with a quick knock on the door, Chintu would appear.

'Chintu, you shouldn't be bringing this kind of thing into the house. What if Amma finds out?' I would protest, while reluctantly opening the magazine to the centre page. It was not so much the athletics of the various couplings that amazed me as the sheer size of the organs in question. When I queried the reason for this, Chintu's stock explanation was always 'it's because they eat chicken every day, not *dal roti* like you and me'.

The first concrete proposal of marriage was brought by none other than Munimji, one of the regulars at Amma's Nehru meetings. A particular favourite of Amma, Munimji resembled an Englishman, with his fondness for high-quality PG Tips tea sent from England by an affectionate niece, and silk cravats which stayed in place even in the height of summer. Gifted with a pale skin, he guarded his complexion with a large navy-blue BOAC umbrella during the summer months. Because he had spent some time in a place called Croydon, during the same period as Nehruji's sojourn at Cambridge, Munimji's remarks were always respected for their authenticity.

On that fateful day, he failed to open his umbrella with the usual aplomb. Amma, noticing this uncharacteristic dilly-dallying and fearing the loss of lifelong membership revenue, tactfully asked him the reason for his discomfiture. Munimji cleared his throat, looked around in confusion, and finally took a small black-and-white photograph out of his wallet. The photograph was of Kamala.

'*Behanji*, your son now seems to be of a suitable age. By the grace of God, he has a gift for words and also a steady government job. This is my maternal aunt's sister-in-law's daughter. She will be like the Joan of Arc in your household, *behanji*,' Munimji concluded with a nervous nod, one hand smoothing the folds of his cravat, a habit which, he was fond of repeating, he shared with none other than Nehruji himself.

Amma was at the time engrossed in some research on Nehruji's marital vicissitudes, in particular the role played in them by Edwina Mountbatten. Mention of the name Kamala therefore seemed startlingly famil-iar. This girl even had the same name as Nehruji's own long-suffering spouse! And, as she explained later, the suggestion that my boat needed a safe harbour struck an immediate chord with her. I was fast approaching my twenty-fifth birthday and she was not particularly happy about the company I was keeping of late, especially that of Sharmila Sharma, who had rung the house once or twice in the evening and boldly asked to speak to me, without so much as a 'Hello. How are you, Auntie?' to her. What guarantee was there that, transformed into such an attractive catch, I would not be ensnared by one of those modern, *filmi* girls who read *Stardust* in their spare time and demanded a colour television and a holiday in Simla every summer?

An image of a fair-petalled rose, very much like Nehruji's own Kamala, floated through Amma's mind. Who knew? Properly trained, she could perhaps one day take over the reins of the Nehru Society, and to top it all it was none other than Munimji who was recommending her. The girl could not come with better references. So enthusiastic was Munimji about Kamala's sterling qualities of sensitivity and simplicity that a passing glance at the photograph was enough to convince Amma.

Much to Father's surprise – he had expected agitated artistic objections to an arranged marriage – I agreed readily to Amma's choice. The timing was perfect for falling in love and being loved back. In one of those startlingly clear moments that illuminate one's entire existence, I saw the years stretching ahead of me with the Sharmila Sharmas of the world continuing to call me 'a good friend' while steadily giving away their hearts and bodies to other, worthless suitors. Besides, there was destiny at work here, for just the day before I had started on one of my most ambitious poetic works to date, a story of star-crossed lovers separated through time and reunited again in death. The heroine could even carry Kamala's physical features.

Rather shyly, I asked Munimji's permission to keep the photograph for a few days. Once, in the privacy of my room, I looked carefully at those large, opaque eyes and the moon-shaped face that gave away nothing. How hard it was to judge the sensitivity of the soul from a passport snapshot.

Being a groom-in-waiting suited me. I took to taking unexplained leave from the office and would wander dreamily among the sleeping tombs and hibiscus bushes of the Lodi Gardens, dreaming of the approaching union. Miss Sinha at the office teased me when sometimes, absent-mindedly, I addressed her as Kamala. Something, though, kept me from breaking the news of my betrothal to my Billo *chaat*-house friends. I already knew what their response would be.

'*Sala*, nothing better to do, now he goes and hangs himself with a petticoat string,' Binoy was sure to say, rolling yet another cigarette.

*

The local community hall just off Rouse Avenue, normally the venue for Red Cross bazaars, wore a festive air that winter evening. Little beaded rivers of light lit up the roof and windows. A *halwai* sat on one side, busily frying hot *puris* and *jalebis,* while a gaggle of over-sequinned girls, all from Kamala's side, stood giggling hysterically in a corner. Uncles and nephews from both families swaggered around with a self-important air, shouting for cold drinks to be brought for the guests and the microphone to be fixed.

Well-meaning wellwishers had hijacked the simple, tasteful wedding Amma and I had anticipated. A motley collection of uniformed men carrying the banner of the Camelot Brass Company were grimly intent on destroying the harmony of the occasion with their rendition of popular *filmi* tunes such as '*Dum Auro Dum*'. Confronted with such competition, the lone violin player Amma had aesthetically placed under the neem tree sulked in silence for the rest of the evening.

The villain of the piece was my grandmother, who was determined that the wedding of her eldest grandson would be a memorable event whose glory would reverberate from Delhi to Kanpur, the town where she normally hibernated for most of the year.

I took an instant dislike to the pandit she had chosen to seal our union. With a large birthmark covering most of his shaven scalp, and bulging, bird-like eyes, he smacked too much of dodgy living to appeal to my ascetic tastes. Much to my annoyance, he obstinately refused to recite the Keats poem I had requested at the end of the ceremony.

'I will be requiring Hindi translation for this. All this English-Vinglish won't do,' he said, callously throwing away the piece of paper.

*

A wedding bed scattered with petals of jasmine and with an auspicious coconut placed on the pillow symbolised the start of my married life. I hesitated a moment before disappearing into the bathroom. Kamala and I were alone at last. Being a typical bashful bride, she'd exchanged no words with me during the ceremony and, with head bowed demurely, had studiously avoided looking at me whenever I tried to catch her eye.

'But what are you doing?' I had come out of the bathroom wearing my new Benarasi silk pyjamas,

41

mouth tingling to the minty taste of Binaca toothpaste, Old Spice aftershave painfully pricking the skin of my armpits.

I'd expected to see my bride crouching timidly on the bed, weeping softly beneath the weight of her heavy red-gold sari. What I saw instead was a stoutish young woman, thin lips pressed together in determination, stripped down to her petticoat and blouse, bent over an open suitcase from which she was purposefully taking out a dozen or so brass statues of Ganesha.

'I can't go to sleep without their blessing,' Kamala replied as she began planting them around the room. Two were placed on the windowsill. My precious books were removed from a shelf to make room for the rest.

'But don't you know? This is a thinking household. We have no place for idols here.'

'These are not idle things but gods. Don't you want their blessings on the sanctity of our marriage?'

Kamala moved swiftly to where I stood, bent down and respectfully touched my feet. 'From this day onwards, you are my lord and master, agreed. I will obey and serve you for the next seven births. All I ask in return is that you don't snatch these gods away from me.'

I found this plea infinitely moving. There was something soft and vulnerable in her entreaty, in the way she instinctively touched my feet. From now on I was to be the guarantor of her future happiness.

'Anything you say, my long-awaited loved one. Look, I wrote this for you, just the other day,' I whispered, handing her a folded piece of paper from my pocket.

Without you . . . my beloved,
There is no fire to the flame,

42

No wing to the bird,
This house remains not a home.

From where I stood I could see the fine hairs at the base of her stomach, just where the red petticoat string cut into the flesh. Her belly button peeped out above it, dark and mysterious. Shamelessly I moved my eyes upward to the ripe outline of her breasts. Their shape seemed so much more substantial than Sharmila Sharma's. Something stirred within me as I thought of Seth's hands that hot summer's day. Gently I pushed Kamala towards the bed, turning on the radio just in case our frantic love cries woke Amma.

*

Kamala and I were profoundly unsuited. There was no other way of phrasing it. How mismatched this well-intentioned union had turned out to be! Not only was she entirely devoid of literary or cultural aspirations, but she was unequivocally opposed to adopting the role of eager disciple. Even more damaging than this was the obsessive religious streak she displayed from time to time, totally unsuitable, as Amma constantly repeated, in a young girl of the twentieth century. Hours were frittered away polishing the brass anklets round Ganesha's feet or preparing carrot *halwa* for Ram Nami. Yet the mere mention of Tennyson or Nehru's Dandi march, and those heavy-hooded eyes would droop and some trivial household or cleaning chore be abruptly recalled.

A state of uneasy truce fell upon the household. Munimji's treachery was discussed at length and Amma even contemplated revoking his NAPS

43

membership. Much to our surprise, it was Father who proved to be Kamala's strongest ally.

'Look here, now,' he said. 'Forget this idea of dismissing Munimji from NAPS or filing a court case against Kamala. What grouse do you really have against the girl? So what if she does not speak good English or could not care less about Nehru? At least she shows our grey hair the respect it deserves. My feet get massaged, you get your bed-tea, and the house is positively tiptop since she took over. Let's not forget that girl's heart is ticking in the right domestic place.'

I think Kamala, for her part, soon realised that, far from being an ideal *bahu*, she had somehow failed our collective expectations. A determined silence came over her then. Always respectful, never demanding, she threw herself with stubborn zeal into running the household and, when our son arrived, into raising him to be a god-fearing, studious child. Her only concession to frivolity was the daily afternoon *kirtan* sessions at the temple nearby, which she insisted on attending.

As for me, it was but another poetic cross to bear. Once the initial shock of being married to a woman more interested in listening to *bhajans* than attending British Council talks on Byron had worn off, I embraced this new life with a shrug of resigned optimism. Wasn't world literature full of epic tales of unfulfilled love? It gave one's verse a certain legitimacy and muscle. Occasionally I speculated about the various romantic possibilities now closed to me for good. This was particularly true on Monday evenings when I took the four o'clock bus home. There was always an excited gaggle of college girls aboard at this time, giggling at the words of a silly *filmi* song, tossing back long dark plaits with smooth, nail-polished hands. Not that I ever contemplated straying. It was a cerebral union I craved, not the mating of two overheated bodies.

As far as nocturnal bodily needs were concerned, once a month or so, fired by the memory of those German magazines from my long-ago boyhood or the proximity of Miss Sinha in the canteen queue, I would discharge my husbandly duties, until Kamala duly obliged by producing a son and heir, Feroze. (Amma insisted on naming him after Nehruji's son-in-law, overruling Kamala, who would have preferred a more devotional name like Hanuman or Ganpati.) Our relations then petered out to a sort of amiable sibling understanding: Kamala left me alone with my scribbling, and I did not question her gods.

Sometimes though, having overslept on a Sunday morning, the romantic song requests on All-India Radio softly humming in the background, I would catch a glimpse of her smooth, firm back arched under the bathroom shower, or the robust motion of the Mysore sandalwood soap slapping against her thigh. A sudden uncurling of desire would come out of nowhere, to dwindle just as quickly as her eyes turned towards me with their shouldn't-you-be-spending-time-with-Feroze? stare.

> *Pale maiden, it is not the fairness*
> *of your cheek I crave*
> *Or the darkness of your hair.*
> *It is not the love-light in your eyes that I need,*
> *but a meeting of true hearts and minds*
> *Fixed upon a single star.*

Amma collapsed in tears of remorse on reading this indication of my feelings and, after diligently making a Hindi translation, left it lying carelessly around the kitchen for Kamala to read and register. It was not until she saw her endeavours being reduced to a paper plane by Feroze that she realised the futility of her actions.

CHAPTER NINE

In print at last

❧

The steady tick-tock of time.
The growing of lines upon one's face.
Friendships strengthened, failures harvested.
The ties of love and duty bruised.
Naidu slowly comes of age.

(Lines from a work in progress, in the style
of Ghalib)

THE PASSING YEARS brought a certain melancholic
maturity and recognition to my verse. No longer
did Sharmila suppress a giggle every time I quoted
a couplet, and even Seth once grudgingly accepted a
submission of mine to the *Illustrated Weekly Views*. The
crowning moment, however, came with the publication
of my first volume, a leather-bound limited edition of
some thirty poems, poignantly entitled *Shipwrecked
Tears*.

The book owed its existence to the kind endeavours of
Miss Sinha, Mr Gupta's brown-eyed steno, who took an
active interest in my parallel career as a poet. It was she
who first suggested the possibilities of self-publishing.

She knew of a certain Mr Mukherjee in Bhopal who specialised in bringing out beautiful, leather-bound editions of poets wishing to sidestep the cutthroat vagaries of the commercial market.

'Just think, sir,' Miss Sinha had said (the respectful 'sir' with which she insisted on addressing me always sent a delicious thrill of power up my spine), 'for a nominal sum you will have the pleasure of seeing your name in print – and at such a tender age, too.'

She could not have been more right. I had by now several years of craftsmanship under my artistic belt and could legitimately aspire to join the ranks of the published. Luckily, Amma was of the same sentiment, and thanks to the kind offices of Miss Sinha (who diligently retyped the whole manuscript in her lunch breaks), my poems were soon dispatched to Bhopal. Mr Mukherjee, we learned by return post, preferred postal order cheques drawn in favour of his Bank of Baroda account at Motihari: 'Further correspondence will only be entertained on receipt of payment.'

'What a Shylock Jew that Mukherjee man is!' Amma exclaimed angrily on reading his letter. 'As though we would go back on our word. Anyway, make sure the cheque is sent by express post this very afternoon.'

'Are you sure, Amma? This will eat away most of our savings,' I protested, for the sum involved, what with extras for binding, dedication and copyright registration, had swollen by a considerable amount. But Amma remained unshaken.

Shipwrecked Tears, with its emotional dedication to my mother ('The strength within my wings') and special mention of Miss Sinha, was ready in less than six months. We were obliged to purchase a certain number of copies and it was a triumph and a pleasure to distribute them to friends and well-wishers. If only Father could have seen this day. But the cruel hand of fate had snatched him just a few months before my book saw the light of day. In a classic case of sour grapes, though, Seth refused to acknowledge the copy I posted to him.

The only other note of envy injected into the proceedings was introduced by Sharmila and company. They were most persistent in demanding to know the identity of the publisher, the royalties involved, the reviews expected and other such tiresome details.

'But why is that trivia important? You have each got your signed copy.' Angrily I pushed the books across the table at Billo's. They were behaving little better than a pack of hunting dogs.

'I think I know what the problem is.' This was Urvashi, insolently drawing on a cigarette in full public view. 'The poor bastard's paid for it himself.'

Shocked by the filthiness of her language, I gathered my books together and left the premises. It was weeks before I could bring myself to approach them again.

The book, as I had anticipated, proved to be but a stepping-stone to further success, for it opened the doors to my first foreign trip abroad – to England, no less, and as a competitor in the prestigious Commonwealth Poetry Competition. It was Amma who first found out the competition details, quite by accident while fiddling with the radio knobs. They were given at the tail end of a Radio Nairobi transmission on irrigation practices in Mombassa.

Amma's face wore a strange glow that day.

'Kavi, this is destiny at work. What better way to reward the sweat and blood you put into *Shipwrecked*

Tears than with a trip to England, the cradle of the English language? Just think, you will be retracing Nehruji's steps, reliving the experiences of Charles Dickens and Wordsworth – with the added prestige of winning an international prize.'

Every waking moment of the following weeks was taken up by Amma plotting ways of getting me to England.

'It will be a pilgrimage for you, Kavi. You will see refinement and civilisation in action. And the English will embrace you as one of their own, for are you not one of their own?'

Before long, using the persuasive cards of her recent widowhood and her charitable work for the Nehru Society, Amma managed to coerce the relevant officials into recognising the necessity of both acknowledging my talent and funding my trip abroad.

'I warned them that India would stagnate unless young blood is let out. "By all means send Seth, Secretary Sahib, but remember it is tomorrow's generation that needs a voice. Our future lies in the hands of these youngsters being appreciated abroad."' Amma conveyed the gist of her conversation with the Joint Secretary of Culture in between triumphant sips of Twinings tea.

With typical bureaucratic secretiveness, though, the Ministry of Culture insisted on maintaining a tight-lipped silence regarding the final shortlist of candidates.

'Security reasons,' the department secretary primly informed me after every telephone call. It took several cups of third-rate tea in their office canteen, and a full crate of export-quality Alfonso mangoes delivered to the Joint Secretary's residence, before I could get her to open her mouth officially. Much to my elation, I learned that Amma's repeated visits to the Ministry had at last paid off. Seth and I were to be the only Indian competitors for the Commonwealth Poetry Competition. And so here I was winging my way to England, suspended twenty thousand feet in the sky, reminiscing nostalgically about my college days, my arty friends, even Kamala.

CHAPTER TEN

England-bound one autumn day

～

UNGAINLY SHAPES LAY belted clumsily to their seats, mouths wide open, eyes shut, limbs sticking out at random like one of those grotesque Ikebana flower arrangements Amma used to do when I was young. Where were the charm and the glamour advertised in those Maharajah posters? If this was the beauty of Air India, economy class, then I, rail-bound for all of my thirty-six years, had not missed much.

The irritating buzz of the plane, the coughing and clearing of throats, and the constant march of harassed mothers and screaming infants to the toilets, soon brought on a headache.

'Please, madam, can I have an Aspro immediately?' I asked one of the air hostesses wandering up and down the aisle. The girl looked blank for a moment, and I noticed that the pleats of her *sari-pallu* were kept in check by a large peacock-shaped brooch.

A thin, reedy, I-would-not-help-you-even-if-I-could voice replied, 'Sorry, sir we are unable to dispense medicine on board. Section 4.3AE of IATA regulations.'

'Well, if it is not too much trouble, can you at least get me some orange juice, no ice cubes, two spoons of sugar and another blanket, please? Are we flying over the North Pole? It is freezing in here.' I hoped the sarcasm in my voice had registered.

The drink and the blanket, needless to say, never materialised. Yet only minutes later the same air hostess, now animated and alert, appeared gliding gracefully towards First Class, bearing a huge cut-glass tumbler of what surely must be straight Scotch and a plate of cashew nuts. They must be for Seth, I reasoned, VIP that he was. But five-star, red-carpet treatment even at 2 a.m.? How typically demanding of the man.

If the bare truth be told, however, I felt immensely honoured to be chosen alongside Seth, the evergreen darling of the literary jet set. His work was regularly serialised in the *New Yorker* and he was only the third Indian to be shortlisted for the Booker twice. No less a person than Sir Trevor Lipton had described him in the *Times Literary Supplement* as an 'eminent giant straddling both East and West'. But fame, I reflected triumphantly, making my way to the toilet at the back of the aircraft, was a great equaliser, for wasn't this self-same Seth now competing for the same honours as me, a modest bureaucrat from the Education Ministry? True, I had been described as 'a poet of some potential' by the Institute of Literary Studies as far back as 1975, but then what was the small-town glory of Delhi compared to the heady applause of New York and London?

A youthful, rather round face with a thick, lustrous head of wavy hair stared back at me from the mirror in the toilet. I had decided soon after reaching thirty that, as far as facial beauty was concerned, my features were never going to achieve Amitabh Bacchan status. That brooding film star was the heartthrob of every Indian woman below the age of sixty. However, there were other qualities of the mind and spirit to compensate. 'That childlike eye', as my friend Sharmila fondly used to say, more than made up for the rather smooth cheeks that needed a shave but once a fortnight, the thick neck, the somewhat pert nose.

'Naidu, such a shame you look more like a small-town trader than a full-blown poet,' Binoy and Sharmila used to say in their taunting moments. I would have preferred to be tall and ethereal, with a lock of silver hair absent-mindedly falling over a noble forehead. A bit like Seth, really. But no, here I was, confined for ever to this modest five-foot-something frame and huge, thick-lashed, sensitive eyes.

I was 'deliciously munchable, like toasted almonds', in Mrs Basu's opinion.

'More like a cud-chewing entity', according to Urvashi, to whom I reported this endearment.

With a sudden drunken lurch, the plane dipped downwards. Breaking off the self-scrutiny, I hastened to my seat as the plaintive sounds of Ravi Shankar's sitar sputtered to life on the audio system. England winked into view, a patchwork of green fields and rows of mousy-brown houses wearing identical neat little red-roof hats. I was struck by the unbroken density of the green, having seldom ventured beyond the perimeters of urban Delhi with its frenzied construction of high-rise buildings and exhaust-fume-clouded trees.

A small, tense fist of excited apprehension slowly uncoiled itself within my belly. So this was England with its rose-patterned curtains, cosy fires and daffodils nodding in the sunshine. Rouse Avenue with its chaotic confusion of dust and flies was left far behind, a postcard memory, and here I stood ready to grab England with hungry arms.

A line from Tennyson crept into my thoughts: 'To strive, to seek, to find, and not to yield.'

But what if I was refused entry on obscure official grounds? Although both Mr Basu and Munimji had carefully explained the strict subtleties of English Immigration rules, there were always hidden footnotes that could be called upon to keep out undesirable aliens. Just the week before my departure, Chintu had teased me that, as a married man with a single male issue, I might need additional reference letters.

'Stop worrying him needlessly,' Amma had replied crossly. 'The English will welcome him with open arms. Don't forget he is a poet, a colleague of Shakespeare and Shelley. In England, they have time for such things.'

I rechecked my passport nervously, flicking through the pages until I came to personal particulars. My eye lingered over the entry 'Occupation: Poet'. This choice of words had led to a rather violent scene with Amma. She'd wanted me to put 'Poet-cum-senior government official', but I preferred to remain loyal to my true vocation. Why hide it from the world?

I patted the official invitation letter nestling in my breast pocket and wiped a piece of fluff from my sleeve. This suit (100 per cent polyester–wool blend), a going-to-glory present from Amma, had to last me a good many years. It was stitched in less than twenty-four hours by no less a tailor than Master Bashir of Chandini Chowk. 'Savile Row-cut, it always suits the Indian gentlemanly pear shape,' he assured me, mouth full of pins, eyes squinting in concentration, running his hands over the cloth as though it were a woman's waist.

Once within the brand-new sparkle of Heathrow Airport, all fatigue and apprehension disappeared. I felt like a child let loose in a toyshop and threw friendly smiles to whoever caught my eye. The airport teemed with fellow Indians, but there was none of the usual lethargic staring into space while one squatted on one's haunches and slowly rolled a *bidi*. Trolleys were being pushed around with ruthless efficiency. Even the babies in their prams seemed to have a known destination in mind. Must be something in the water, I decided, while here I was, lingering aimlessly, taking pains to read every neon-lit advertising sign. Suddenly the world was an Alfonso mango, ripe for the plucking.

Far in the distance I could see the tall figure of Seth purposefully carving his way through the crowds, the folds of his pashmina shawl flapping round him as he waved his hands about in that theatrical fashion.

Soon it was my turn to face the immigration desk. I decided on a confident, familiar approach. 'Beautiful airport. Newly built?'

'Will you be here long, sir? a cut-glass voice asked from behind a plastic screen.

'I hope it will be a long, fruitful stay.' It was, I instantly realised, the wrong reply to make.

The voice inside the booth became a touch more cut-glass. 'I need to see your documents, sir.'

'Why? Isn't Her Majesty's visa good enough?' was my witty repartee. I had rehearsed this phrasing countless times with Mr Basu.

'I'm afraid not, sir. Now, may I see the invitation letter?' A note of weariness had crept into his voice.

This was my moment of triumph. I watched him read the invitation from the Organising Committee and reach thoughtfully for the rubber stamp.

In years to come, I reflected, walking towards the baggage claim, that humble clerk would tell the grandchildren perched upon his knee that it had been his privilege to welcome Kavi Naidu to the shores of England.

I soon espied Seth by the relevant luggage belt. 'I saw you were having a bit of trouble with that immigration officer. Sorry I couldn't be more helpful,' I heard myself mumbling. Seth had that effect on people.

'On the contrary, the chap had read my last book and wanted an autograph. Surprising, really. You wouldn't expect the clerical sort to have the sensibility to comprehend a metaphysical post-modern work.' Seth spoke in his usual mellifluous voice, which was more River Isis than River Ganges.

His suitcase, a dignified leather affair tattooed with innumerable foreign labels, was the first to arrive. 'Well, bound to see you around sometime,' he said dismissively, deftly wheeling his trolley out through the exit gate where a glamorous-looking English couple, she big-boned and with shiny yellow hair, engulfed him in a ferocious embrace, the woman cooing all the time like an over-excited pigeon.

Suddenly I wanted to be home with my own cooing pigeons. If one took into account Indian Standard Time, this would be the precise moment when I would usually be emerging from my evening bath, wearing the starched pyjamas that Kamala would have hung just within reach of the bathroom door.

She, of course, would be diligently polishing the statues of Lord Ganesha that supervised our nightly sleep from a shelf just below the bedroom window – 'Like us, even the gods need to feel tiptop before their sleep' was her standard explanation. Meanwhile, Amma in the kitchen would be boiling my tea to the right strength, adding the crushed cardamom just as the water came to the boil. There was no question about it; back home I was the King of the Castle.

Here I was an anonymous speck in a steady stream of foreigners whizzing past me with no trace of friendly recognition. There was no sign of any welcoming High Commission official, and I was just about to report myself to the Lost and Found counter when a bright yellow banner bearing the legend 'KAVI NAIDU' caught my eye.

'You being the poetry gentleman?' the bearer of the board asked me in a low, suspicious whisper. It was Gonzales, the High Commission driver.

*

London greeted me – a slap of cold drizzle and a bewildering confusion of grey high-rises and rows and rows of shops, many, I was amazed to note, bearing Indian names. What was even more impressive was the orderly way in which the traffic circulated round the neat round-abouts, where there was not a single beggar or cow in sight. 'What well-mannered people!' I exclaimed to Gonzales as he expertly overtook a large double-decker bus without provoking so much as a honk or an obscenely-worded insult from the smiling African driver.

We soon reached the place where I was staying. The Ascension Modern Hotel was a modest affair, apologetically tucked between two much grander buildings – and there I was with visions of five-star air-conditioned opulence. My mood, however, perked up when Gonzales informed me that this was the celebrated West End, the heart of artistic London, and that the Indian High Commission lay but a stone's throw away. My spirits sank again as we entered the hotel lobby, which smelled of fried coconut. Colourful posters of the Taj Mahal and Rajasthan hung in cheap plastic frames all along the turquoise-painted walls. A brass filigree lamp threw criss-cross shadows on the faded Kashmiri rug on the floor. How was I expected to imbibe English culture when surrounded by such *desi* paraphernalia? The hotel, in fact, looked empty and lonely, what with the open doors and the little cleaning trolleys parked in the corridors on a semi-permanent basis.

The manager, one Mrs Pereira, came rushing out from behind the desk to greet us, her face garlanded with smiles, plastic slippers making a quiet plopping against the green linoleum floor. She was, I later learned, the second cousin of Gonzales.

'Welcome to England, Mr Kavi. Welcome to the land of Keats and Shelley.'

How had she guessed my vocation? I instantly warmed to her.

'I hope you enjoy your stay here.'

Mrs Pereira had one of those faces that never sit still: dark, pointed, held together by the fiercest set of eyebrows I had ever seen. Round her neck dangled a blue satin ribbon holding a huge mother-of-pearl cross. This clashed dramatically with her orange housecoat printed with green dragons.

'Could this be your personal albatross?' I pointed to the cross, confident of her poetic insight.

'Evangelical Syrian-Christian' was the prompt reply. 'All meals to be consumed in the dining hall, punctual sharp. Hot beverages can be provided on a twenty-four-hour basis at an additional cost, but no alcoholic intoxicants on the premises,' she continued while leading me to my room.

'Oh, there is no danger of that.' I laughed self-deprecatingly. 'I happen to be a strict teetotaller. Moreover, I don't eat meat on Tuesdays and no pork at any time in deference to my wife's religious feelings.' But it was obvious that this insight into my personal eating preferences was of little interest to her.

Suddenly I wanted her to be friendly, to show an interest in my private pursuits. Gonzales had disappeared by then, after whispering a hoarse 'seven o'clock' into my ear. This, I assumed, was the time he would be picking me up for the welcoming reception at the Indian High Commissioner's residence.

'Tell me, Mrs Pereira, how did you guess I was a poet?'

Her face hinted at a deeper spiritual awareness. Perhaps this hotel job was just a front. I debated showing her my poems. They were there, sewn into the inner lining of my suitcase. Amma did not want them falling into unscrupulous customs hands.

'Oh, that was easy. I am not born tomorrow, you know. This is how the reservation was made by those Commonwealth people. Now you will excuse me, I must attend to the other guests.'

I used another delaying tactic. 'The hotel seems empty. Business not good?' There was sympathy in my voice.

'Not good?' Mrs Pereira's eyebrows looked at me scornfully. 'Just wait a few days, term will start again at that LSE.' Her chin pointed in a general south-easterly direction. 'And then you will see, the place will be crawling with scholarly types begging for a room. I still give the best bedding rates in town.' The eyebrows returned to their triumphant position. She considered me carefully. 'Now, please, I will be requiring your passport for safe-keeping.' And with an abrupt nod she was gone.

The room was unremarkable and shabby. I was intrigued by the presence of a washbasin and an Indian edition Bible, placed helpfully beside the bed, and almost rang Mrs Pereira to seek an explanation. The window looked out on an unused alleyway where a thin figure sat drinking by a makeshift fire. This window, most worryingly, refused to shut completely after I had finished my inspection of the outer world. But these were minor hiccups, I comforted myself. I was here not to set up headquarters but to win long-awaited recognition. The important thing was to make the place as homely as I could. First came the photograph of Feroze taken on a school trip to Darjeeling. This I propped on the bedside stool. Next came *Shipwrecked Tears* and *Roget's Thesaurus,* and the bright blue plastic mug that Amma, with her usual foresight, had insisted on packing.

'The English do not use water like us after answering the call of nature. They use paper, most *junglee*-like, so you had better take this mug,' she had muttered disapprovingly.

Now only the poems remained. I took out the scissors hidden in my breast pocket and, with what I

61

considered a deft hand, neatly sliced the lining of the suitcase in two. The poems, all one hundred and sixty-two of them, lay resting in their virginal folder of pure raw silk. The first poem I took out was the one I had written on Oxford, inspired by a print I had seen in a bookshop near Billo's.

> *Dreaming of your ancient spires,*
> *This hapless dreamer sighs in pain.*
> *The chiming of your ageless bells,*
> *The slow foot-fall of falling rain*
> *For ever will their memory course through my veins.*

True, the poem had not attracted as wide or appreciative a reception as I had anticipated when it initially appeared in the *Indian Express*. Indeed, Seth had mocked it as just the latest Wordsworthian diatribe to bite the twentieth-century dust. Well, the next few days were going to be full of nasty surprises for him. It was not so much that I was trying to convince myself; I had a strong premonition that the prize was destined to be mine.

*

The High Commissioner's residence, a palatial mansion hidden behind a sea of green, was guarded by tall iron gates and a camera which eyed me critically at the door. A blur of twinkling chandeliers, expensive Persian rugs and nude marble statues swam before my eyes. Enormous potted ferns dotted around the room gave it the feel of a tropical paradise. A large black-and-white portrait of an unsmiling Gandhiji at his spinning wheel presided gloomily over this lavish display.

Even time proceeded more efficiently in England. I was the first guest to arrive. Only a few waiters were loitering in the reception hall, carrying platters of delicious-smelling food to an immensely long table. I was suddenly aware of the urgent rumblings of my belly. I had not eaten anything since my arrival that morning. All decorum forgotten, I rapidly advanced towards the samosas on the banquet table, to be stopped in mid-flight by a hand placed on my shoulder.

'Why, you must be one of our distinguished visiting artists,' a suave voice addressed me. 'I do apologise for not welcoming you earlier.'

It was none other than His Excellency Mr Mistry, the High Commissioner himself, a tall distinguished-looking man with a goatee beard and deep, searching eyes fixed on my face.

'Honoured to meet you, Your Majesty,' I said in confusion. 'Kavi Naidu at your service. I am here to receive the prize, sir.'

'But the pleasure is mine. Both my wife and I take an avid interest in the arts and rarely miss an opportunity to encounter the creative spirit that moves them all,' his cultured tones informed me.

Such courtly language, such noble sentiments! Just like the English aristocracy. Nobody in my life had ever engaged me in such intellectual high-flown talk, not even my Billo *chaat*-house friends, always ready with cutting barbs whenever I started musing about creativity.

'*Sala* Naidu,' they would say. 'His hormones are playing up again.' If only they could see me now.

'Let us see,' I said, 'what happens when the awards are announced this week. It may be that your humble servant may be able to place a trophy at your feet.' I stopped in confusion, for Mr Mistry had vanished.

The hall was gradually filling up and I could make out the tall figure of Seth holding court among a babble of excited African ladies. It was always the women he picked on, the weakest link in the human chain. I decided to remain in splendid isolation, still savouring my recent triumph. Let the needy network. My thoughts returned to the samosas.

For the second time that evening, a voice stopped my progress. 'My husband has been telling me all about you. I am Naina – I insist you call me that. This is your first trip abroad, isn't it?'

I found myself being gently nudged towards a velvet sofa by an extremely elegant woman.

Naina Mistry was a good head taller than me, with heavy dark-brown hair tied in an elaborate bun and the reddest lips I had ever seen. Her sari, of some shimmering material, did amazing things to her eyes, making them now brown, now green, even as we spoke. Never had I seen such material before, certainly not on Kamala or Amma, who stuck respectively to stiff, starched cottons and prim, subdued silks. This lady looked utterly female, even though she was my senior by a good many years.

I felt twice-privileged that evening, and gratefully accepted the pink-toned liquid she so kindly pressed upon me. It was not sherbet but alcohol. The realisation came a split second too late. Less than twenty-four hours after leaving India, the childhood vow to my father had been broken. Soon I would be chewing beef and sleeping with white women. A little tear of remorse wound its way down my cheek.

Madam looked at me, puzzled, and with an extremely touching gesture, wiped away the tear with the end of her *sari-pallu*.

'You poets are such emotional creatures,' she murmured, patting my hand and leaning understandingly towards me. The folds of her sari accidentally slipped away, revealing a pale, smooth neck which led to a heavy bosom straining against the sheer fabric of her blouse.

'Madam, I have never touched alcohol before. I have broken a promise.'

'Oh, so regretful! But don't you find there is something so delicious in breaking promises? Surely as a poet you must be accustomed to drinking. How else do you start the fire in your belly . . . to write of love and passion?' A low, musical laugh accompanied her words.

I was speechless, unable to take my eyes away from the throbbing vision of womanhood in front of me. Her Excellency continued the conversation in the same effortless way, enquiring about my job, my family, and the state of the traffic in Delhi. She herself had lived there till the age of fourteen, she informed me, after which she had been packed off to a tedious boarding school in Simla run by Irish nuns, who thought nothing of making the girls bare their bottoms, under the cold December moon as a punishment for reading Mills and Boon.

'Darling, so you have discovered our local poet. Isn't he delightful?' Mr Mistry had reappeared by our side.

'Yes, there is something so fresh and unedited about him.' Madam's voice rose excitedly, and for a moment I thought they would both pat my head approvingly.

'I know, I know, but we must not forget the other guests, dear.' A hand reached out almost imperceptibly and returned the *sari-pallu* to its original position.

What a handsome couple they made, no pomp, no snobbery, to single me out thus. The affectionate way in which Madam had said she would be sending for me soon to show me the sights . . . Really, it was beyond the call of duty. I tried to memorise the kind words they had spoken, and eagerly looked around for Seth to inform him of my diplomatic conquest.

I must have got up too suddenly, for the room began to swing gently and the rumblings in my stomach turned to an urgent knocking. Before I knew it, I was lying foetal-fashion on the floor clutching a potted fern leaf for support. The last thing I remembered was Mr Mistry's voice calling for a doctor and Madam instructing a guard to carry me upstairs to the blue guest-room.

CHAPTER ELEVEN

The blue guest-room

~

Like a moth fluttering
between two lights.
The moon and the sparkle
within your eyes.
O beloved, set me free
from this torment
before I burn my wings in haste.

(From an unpublished poem)

THE NEXT THING I knew, two sturdy arms were
swinging me past an amused-looking Seth, past the
twittering plumage of the African ladies and up the
sweeping staircase copied straight out of *Gone with the
Wind*, where I respectfully greeted Gandhi's portrait
before disappearing into the guest-room.

The room was dark and velvety. Huge gilt mirrors
threw back my reflection from every wall, and blue
brocade curtains sealed out the world. The bed was
one of those unending, sinful affairs more fitting for
the amorous pursuits of a loving couple than for the
stomach cramps of a hungry poet.

'I really am all right. It is merely a question of food, then I will be ready to rejoin the festivities,' I pleaded to the burly Gurkha resolutely tucking me into bed. I would have slaughtered a herd of holy cows for one of Mrs Basu's fish curries.

And the evening had begun so well. Not only had I held Mr Mistry's privileged ear, but even the First Lady had hung on my every word, and then I had to go and ruin it all by a stupid fainting fit. A small lump rose within my throat. This was hardly the right introduction to the English high life. As if on cue, Amma's parting words at the airport came back: 'Never forget, son, the blessed silver lining that ties you to every cloud.' The wording may have been inexact, but the wisdom was all there.

Viewed from that maternal angle, the evening was perhaps not such a failure. My absence would have provoked a wave of concerned interest down below. Anxious guests were even now flocking around Mr Mistry, demanding to know the state of my health. Grim parallels were being drawn. Hadn't Keats died of consumption? Soon a hearty English doctor, Dickensian and bluff with silver-grey whiskers, would bring the might of British medicine to my aid. And Seth? I allowed myself the briefest of smiles. Merely a footnote to all this. With one single deft fall, I had become the centrepiece of the evening.

I drifted off into a troubled sleep in which the aroma of chicken biryani competed with Seth's laughter filtering into the room like some noxious fume. Some time later — it must have been nearly morning, judging from the pale light leaking through the curtains — the door opened and an indistinct form floated towards my bed.

Long, spider-like fingers brushed my cheek and wandered speculatively through my hair. A most intimate way of examining, these English doctors had. Perhaps it was their way of making me feel at ease.

'We missed you last night. I was so keen on you reciting a poem.' A familiar silky fabric fell on my face. Shock! It was none other than Mrs Mistry, still attired in that shimmering sari and smelling strongly of some alcoholic beverage. There was nothing to do but yelp in surprise.

'Shush, now! We would not want to wake up the entire household, would we? My husband happens to be an extremely light sleeper.'

With these warning words, the bedspread was delicately pushed aside as with one swift movement, surprisingly athletic for such a big woman, Mrs Naina Mistry joined me in bed. I could smell the drink from where I lay, and the talcum powder sprinkled within her cleavage dripped like pale punctuation marks onto my shirt. I heard her breathing beside me: short, sharp and urgent.

Amma's homilies, Kamala's gods, even my second-class degree in Comparative Literature from Kishori Mal College, had not prepared me for this: the amorous advances of an unknown, determined woman. I desperately needed the toilet . . . but how?

'I hope you are aware of your doings on . . .' Faced with the seriousness of the situation, my grasp of English grammar deserted me momentarily.

'You really are being a tease, Naidu. Stop acting bewildered. All you poets are the same . . . lustful creatures that you are.' And tweaking my ear playfully, she commenced nibbling my throat. 'How interesting, you smell of mothballs. A new aftershave?'

69

How could I tell her it was my blazer, which had remained wrapped in splendid isolation for the past dozen years?

Nothing she did that night could compare to the chaste marital embraces I normally exchanged with Kamala, amorous manoeuvres delicately conducted with our backs turned to Lord Ganesha. 'Remember, I am only going through this for the sake of a son', was Kamala's standard come-on line on those rare occasions when I approached her as a man would a woman. How I wished my *chaat*-house friends could see me now, being stroked and chewed by such a highly distinguished woman. Despair and a heady realisation of self-worth fought within my conscience. For the second time in my life, I fainted.

A million light-years later, Naina was still there, one hand tapping restlessly on my chest.

'How terribly Victorian of you to faint just then. Tell me, how could one resist such a bashful plea?'

Her voice, soothing, unintelligible, washed over me like one of those shipping forecasts on the BBC World Service. More worryingly, her hands had become creatures in their own right, running over my body and pausing at just the right lumps and bumps.

'Ah, Naidu . . . how long it is since I have broken into untried flesh.'

And before I knew it, my head lay cradled between those ample milk-bearing glands, and my muscle of manhood was being expertly fondled into life. Not since the creation of Feroze had it seen such action.

She was a passionate woman, I will not deny that; a woman fit for a Byron. As for me, I was merely a humble tool in the hand of higher forces.

Somewhere in the darkness a clock chimed. I forced my eyes open and looked up. Gone was the diplomatic poise of the evening before. The kohl round Mrs Mistry's eyes had left fingerprint bruises all over her cheeks. The *jamun*-red ripeness of the lips was faded and an untidy pool of saliva clung to her chin. Her hair, having come undone sometime during the night, drooped like a tired strand of rope over her shoulder.

What part had I played in this humiliating though enjoyable adventure? Following primeval instinct, I lay curled on the bed, still naked. For some reason, I remembered the time when Feroze had caught malaria. The doctors advised calling an ambulance but Kamala, with her own peculiar brand of obstinacy, refused to give up. For five days and nights she went without food and water, and on the fifth day Feroze opened his eyes. Such was the moral strength of a semi-literate woman, and this was mine, a puppet ready to dance to the tune of the first available woman. I felt like weeping, but even tears, usually such trusted allies, betrayed me that night.

> *A mother's love, a wife's trust,*
> *like a blinding sword*
> *they cut through the night,*
> *forcing even the gods to lower their eyes.*

I had failed both wife and mother. What right did I have to be the author of such noble lines?

*

Mr Mistry paid a visit to the blue guest-room the next morning. Accompanying him was a thin,

71

worried-looking boy who he introduced as the High Commission doctor.

'This has been most unfortunate, Mr Naidu, but please don't worry. Dr Patel here will give you a thorough check-up. I have no doubt you will be on your feet before long. I must remind them to send up your breakfast. Usually Naina does all this, but she has one of her headaches.'

Intelligent, concerned eyes looked at me. A warm hand patted me on the shoulder. How could that woman betray such a man? My tears came flowing thick and fast.

'Come, come, we mustn't give in to despair.' Mr Mistry patted me again, as he would a son. 'Remember, you are among friends here, besides being an envoy of Indian culture.'

I had an overwhelming urge to confide in him then and there – 'Your Excellency, I have been indecently assaulted by your wife' – but stopped at the last minute. It would be wrong to crush a man of such stature.

Dr Patel, thoughtfully fingering his stethoscope, was staring at my chest, which was an angry criss-cross of scratches. 'The mosquitoes must be bad. I thought the monsoons were over in India,' he mumbled before pronouncing himself satisfied with my condition.

'Just jet lag. A day's rest should cure it. However, if I were you I would prolong it. It is not every day that one gets to be a VIP house guest.' He smiled enviously.

VIP guest indeed! I would have been far better protected and fed in a one-room *jhuggi* in East Delhi. Couldn't the man see I hadn't been fed since noon yesterday, and had been violated as well?

*

72

Once back at the hotel, I refused to leave my room for the next two days. A perturbed Mrs Pereira, her celebrated eyebrows curled in concern, kindly proposed a clandestine bottle of black-label Scotch.

'Guaranteed cure for homesick blueness,' she assured me, furtively fingering her cross and looking suspiciously around the room for tell-tale signs of a man on the brink of a breakdown. A strategically placed razorblade, some pills upon the pillow.

'Remember, now, no open drinking in the lobby. I am all too familiar with the hanky-panky behaviour of you poets.' Her tone was authoritative. 'One minute all smiles and the next I'll be ringing Hounslow cemetery for a spot. Just you remember, now, this is a God-abiding hotel. Scandals find no room here.'

If only she knew, the poor misguided soul! It was not the clarion call of mortality that was beckoning Kavi Naidu, but a storm of another description. I refused her offer of the alcohol, quietly, firmly. And no, I didn't want to put my name down for the special evening tour of the Queen's jewels at that London Tower. Weren't they Indian, anyway? Now, if she would excuse me, I had lines to scribble, thoughts to discipline, before they fled. And Horlicks at night would be quite adequate.

Having brusquely dismissed her, I sat down on the bed and reconsidered for the tenth time that fateful reception. My first evening in England, and I had been physically and emotionally abused, and by a fellow Indian, too. What other kinds of danger was I exposing myself to in this foreign country? I debated whether a bath could erase the confusion hanging like an oversized cobweb within my head, and decided against it. It was much too soon to face nakedness of any sort. So, pulling a blanket round my shoulders, I decided on a concrete line of action: a letter to Mrs Naina Mistry on that lovely Japanese rice-paper Miss Sinha had given me for my last birthday.

'Dear Mrs Mistry' – the married credentials a firm reminder of the gravity of her actions – 'Let these words be my crutches when all else fails . . .'

Far too melodramatic, and a letter could easily fall into the wrong hands. Giving up, I listened to Mrs Pereira hoovering her way down the corridor. My vows to Kamala, to Feroze, to Amma, lay scattered around me like 'the torn eyes of a peacock's plumage'. The words of Swinburne came to mind. I thought regretfully of the competition and my poems. There was no option but to catch the next flight home, if only to preserve my dignity against further indecent assaults.

And let Seth walk away with the prize? Never. I could not let Amma down. For her sake I would rise again like a phoenix and restore my visit to its rightful purpose. My molestation by Mrs Mistry would remain just that, an ugly English escapade to be relived in selected anonymous poems. How was I to know that destiny had other designs on me? Virginal for most of my life, little did I know that I was being drawn to a different kind of fire, the kind that lurked within those distant boyhood German magazines?

*

'A parcel for you, sir.' Gonzales stood outside, holding a silver box. Inside the parcel, which I opened with trembling fingers, lay a single red rose and a message: 'Practice makes perfect. Tell me when?'

I was doomed. Mrs Mistry was determined never to set me free.

The next days passed in a giddy blur. A smirking Gonzales escorted me punctually to the Mistrys' residence every morning and delivered me into Mrs Mistry's capable, waiting hands.

I tried several times to make my intentions daylight clear, but without success. 'Please leave this family man alone. Don't distract me from my true vocation. What will Amma or the world say?' I would entreat beseechingly, but Mrs Mistry simply waved aside my protestations with a laugh.

These hectic, amorous ambushes almost always took place in her private study. It was an intimate room where the dark maroon walls glowed with illustrations of cavorting couples in various stages of disrobement. The curtains were always drawn and the table lamps remained lit even in broad daylight. Mrs Mistry would receive me like a queen, sitting erect on the edge of a comfortable leather armchair. Her favourite mode of attire for these clandestine encounters was a transparent Tibetan-style caftan, through which the outlines of her naked, athletic limbs were clearly visible. One bare foot tapped continually against the Persian carpet with its design of two Greek-looking figures engaged in wrestling.

Kamala, Feroze, even Amma, seemed a lifetime away. My thoughts, all one hundred per cent of them, were numbed by those caramel-coloured lips devouring me.

'Mrs Mistry, I believe this can only go by the name of love. You have finally met a kindred spirit. But please realise there are far too many taboos against such a union. I happen to be a happily married man,' I heard myself reasoning with her, while removing her hand from beneath my clothing.

A loud, inarticulate sound met this declaration. Mrs Mistry was moved, no doubt about it. Helpless tears rolled down her cheeks, she clutched her sides in pain. I was right: here was a Genevieve crying out to be rescued by a Galahad.

'You pillock!' Not being familiar with the word, I took it as a form of colloquial English endearment. 'Do you honestly believe . . . ?' Unable to continue, in a rush of emotion she abruptly pushed me away.

'Button up now. You look bloody ridiculous with that bloody pot belly hanging out.' What a contradiction she was, compared to Kamala's wholesome duffer-like simplicity. I would have to use all the poetic intuition at my disposal to extricate myself from her Medusa-like grip.

'So how confident of winning this poetry prize are you?' Naina questioned me one morning, all carnal craving gone. We were in the formal drawing room. A plate of sandwiches lay by her side, and some Western classical music twittered in the background. I suddenly felt at a disadvantage.

'Sexual encounters always leave me ravenous,' she confided, reaching out for a sandwich without bothering to offer me any. The use of the plural bothered me slightly. Surely I was the only one? After her husband, of course.

'So you really think you can make it?' I could hardly believe that cold, assessing voice belonged to the same woman as the one I had heard panting in the study earlier.

'Naina, there is but one obstacle that stands between the prize and me.' I hesitated before pronouncing the name: 'Seth.' There was everything to be gained by being frank.

'Seth? Of course. He's terribly accomplished, is he not? And so well endowed. Bound to make mincemeat of you.'

I did not like the way she spoke with her mouth full, and conceded this reluctantly. But then, she had not actually read any of my poems. Her overwhelming passion continually got in the way.

'Don't pull such a long face, my Naidino. There is one way of tipping the scales in your favour. We must expose you to the media.' Naina looked doubtful as she said this, then brightened instantly.

'I know what will do the trick. A lunch in your honour at Chez Gerard. Even the Royals have to fight to get a booking there. I'll pull together a few of the literary heavyweights and get my secretary to leak the news to the *Tittle-Tattle*.

I smiled, infected by her enthusiasm. 'But would not a serious interview with the BBC or *The Times* be more appropriate? What is this tattle-vattle, anyway?'

'Listen, do you want to be a celebrity or not? Then let me handle the short cuts. As it is, we might have left it a bit late.'

'Have left what a bit late, my dear?' Standing at the door were none other than His Excellency Mr Mistry and Seth, who was staring at me in a peculiar fashion.

CHAPTER TWELVE

A conversation in the park

~

MR MISTRY AND Seth's sudden return startled me. Naina, however, lost none of her composure and continued munching her sandwiches, the only sign of unease being one bare toe going tip-tap against the floor. Seth took one look at us, raised an enquiring eyebrow and then commenced prowling around the room, peering at the Mughal miniatures in what I took to be a most inquisitive fashion.

Abruptly, out of the blue, he suggested a walk in St James's Park. 'A constitutional to clear the senses, Naidu. I believe you may well have taken leave of them,' he remarked with a sneer.

Under ordinary circumstances, this invitation would have thrown me into a frenzy of grateful excitement, but recent events, namely Mrs Mistry's newly acquired passion for me, had altered that. I could now play the confident, inaccessible card.

'We'll have to see, Seth. Naina – I mean, Mrs Mistry – has drawn up such a hectic schedule for me. She is planning to launch my talent here in England. There is so much to be organised, so little time.' My shoulders rose helplessly as I threw a discreet glance at Naina, who was deeply engrossed in a low-toned conversation with Mr Mistry. A long, convoluted explanation justifying my presence, no doubt.

'Launch?' Seth took up my remark. 'You make yourself sound like a rocket – or perhaps a comet was what you had in mind?'

Never before had I been the recipient of so many unsolicited words from Seth. The Mistrys, meanwhile, sat in the farthest corner of the room – in fact, the very alcove where Naina had first displayed her charms to me. She was stroking her husband's arm, which lay like a docile puppy in her lap. Little inarticulate bubbles of sound rose periodically from her throat. Mr Mistry's eyes were firmly shut, and now and again he gave a violent tug to his goatee beard, no doubt an expression of immense bliss.

'Don't they make a delightful duet, Naidu?' Seth pointed in the Mistrys' direction. 'Touching, isn't it? And to think they've been married for twenty years. Any minute now you and I will have the privilege of assisting in the first diplomatic re-enactment of the *Kama Sutra*.'

With a sardonic chuckle he rose from his seat and made for the door. 'Come now, Naidu, don't look so positively alarmed. Not quite your average Delhi drawing-room scene, is it? Let's go for that walk before – how did that ridiculous poem of yours go? – "The flames of passion consume us all?" '

Seth's lighthearted banter confused me no end, as did Naina's inexplicable behaviour. There she was exchanging sweet nothings with her husband, when barely an hour before our flesh had melted as one. I took up Seth's invitation with gratitude. It would give me an opportunity to buy a few postcards for Feroze. His hobby was collecting views of famous international monuments and Big Ben was missing from the English series. And Kamala? It didn't bear thinking about. The serpent of remorse reared its ugly head within my breast. I threw a reproachful look at Naina. With an absent-minded wave, the unusually amorous couple shooed us off, Naina smiling dreamily while Mr Mistry played with her buttons.

Seth and I were soon speeding through London in the diplomatic limousine. The remarkable change in his demeanour further bewildered me. Here we were, sitting and conversing together as equals with Seth helpfully pointing out the wide avenues, the horseback guards in front of the palaces, etc. Yet in Delhi he would not even deign to spit at me. Perhaps he had got wind of my status as Mrs Mistry's new soulmate and was keen to get a glimpse into the inner circle. The balance of power was clearly shifting. I listened quietly to his touristic explanations and then politely pointed out that my life membership of the North Indian branch of the British Council had made me more than familiar with the vagaries of British history. Only last month, I had brought myself up to date on the origins of the War of the Roses. Besides, wasn't Delhi itself teeming with all this imperial paraphernalia?

Seth puzzled me. He was actually taking the trouble of sharing the same seat and pocket of air as me. Surely there was 'something black in the lentil soup', as Amma would say. She always made a point of giving a literal English translation of Indian sayings for the benefit of Kamala, who, having but a Higher Secondary pass in Hindi, needed to be made aware of the subtleties of the English language. Amma happened to be one of the first female postgraduates in Political History in the country. Her dissertation, on 'The Impact of Nehru upon the Indian Nationalist Movement, with Special Reference to Bengal', occupied pride of place on our drawing-room bookshelf. Just her luck, then, to be saddled with a daughter-in-law who refused to eat garlic on Tuesdays and insisted on a private chat with Lord Ganesha before bed.

'Your thoughts seem to have flown homewards, Naidu. These foreign climes probably don't suit your limited domestic tastes. Why, you're scarcely paying attention to the phallic thrust of Nelson's Column.'

What diction, what articulation: a wordsmith of the highest order. I ran out of superlatives and gazed at Seth in silent admiration. Was he a mind-reader as well?

Now he would be thinking I was a homesick little sparrow longing to fly back to the nest. It was important to shift the conversation to a higher plane. What better way than to talk of his latest book?

'I thoroughly enjoyed *A Fractured Map: An Accusation*. I think you handled the "post-colonial angst of the main protagonist" beautifully.' Thank God I had memorised that *Times of India* quote.

'But how can you have enjoyed it, Naidu? It doesn't come out till late next year, and I doubt whether Ostrich, my publishers, sent you an advance copy.' Seth looked surprised.

'Well, it must have been Simon Rushton's review in *The Times*, then. And isn't Moscow interested in it also?'

It was important to keep the tone light, bright and envy-free as we casually wandered over to a bench and sat down. Seth's singular success in securing the sale of

TV and film rights for almost all his books was a source of unending resentment in the artistic circles within which I moved in Delhi. Spiteful rumours of a cargo of virgins being stealthily delivered to the relevant producer's couch regularly did the rounds of Billo's *chaat*-house. All sour grapes, really, to which I paid no heed. My concerns were of a higher nature and I now proceeded to voice them.

'Besides, if I may be frank, strictly as one intellect to another, I do not agree with all your English-bashing in the book. Don't you think this colonial guilt business has been milked to death?' I wanted Seth to know that I, too, was familiar with the political concepts of the day.

There was a long, uncomfortable pause during which he observed the surrounding foliage with rapt concentration.

'I find English parks too mild and good-natured,' Seth observed, half speaking to himself. 'No danger of snakes or damn bats swiping at you inside half-eaten tombs.'

I quite agreed with him. St James's Park was pretty and picturesque in a feminine kind of way, a bit like a Bombay film set, with wide-eyed flowers peeping from every corner and weeping willows trailing their long necks over the water. Even the ducks waddled around with docile familiarity, the little bands round their feet like friendly dog-collars.

'The point is, Naidu, though for obvious reasons I don't expect you to understand' – Seth had at last decided to address my intellectual concerns – 'contemporary Indian consciousness has been wounded for ever by the colonial symbiosis. What does your average Mr Patel now hanker after most? McDonald's and Mercedes, while his children masturbate to the slow strut of the BeeGees behind closed doors. Any post-modern writer worth his balls needs to take this malaise of Western materialism into account.'

Seth continued without waiting for a reply: 'It's all very well to write of the anguish of lovers parting and birds and bees fornicating among the bushes.' Pointedly he looked at me. 'But that is merely an infinitesimal hiccup in worldwide cyclical terms, you understand? It is high time such third-rate paper-wasters realised the limitations of their craft.' Long, sensitive fingers stressed each point by stabbing the air.

His words were painful. This long diatribe was nothing but a sneaky full-frontal attack. Was this the intention behind our walk? What better place to inflict such a wound than a half-deserted park at nightfall. A 'hiccup'? My untold years of unwavering devotion to poetry had been reduced to that? A poem rose spontaneously to my lips:

> 'Lovers heed not the coldness of this world.
> No shoulder to weep on,
> No hand to hold.
> Unloved will you wander
> Through the changing wheels of time.'

It was the juxtaposition of 'lovers' with 'unloved' that Amma particularly appreciated. The poignancy was, however, lost on Seth, who gave a loud laugh and leaning towards me offered me a cigarette.

'My dear Naidu, ever ready to bounce back with the *mot juste.*'

The metallic chilliness of the bench slowly seeped through my underclothes. More infuriatingly, I was unable to come up with a suitable form of retaliation. Arm flung back, Seth puffed away contentedly at his French cigarette. His wounding words mocked me afresh. There was only one way to retaliate. I could in a subtle, discreet manner hint at a liaison of immense importance – which would shake the God from his pedestal.

'They are a charming couple, Mr Mistry and his wife, so scholarly and artistic. You probably don't know them very well.' Casually phrased observations, just flung in mid-air.

'Not know them?' Seth exploded in anger. 'I could tell you the exact number of hairs on their backs.'

I chose to ignore this childish bragging. 'She is so much like an artist's muse, isn't she?' It was an open-ended compliment designed to open further infor-mational doors.

'Muse!' Seth snorted contemptuously. 'That's Naina for you. She has perfected the art of looking intelligent without actually being so. You know how they met, of course?'

Before I could reply he went on, 'She was nothing but a two-bit air hostess with a tinpot airline – Air Mauritius I think it was – and he was returning from some high-level chinwag. She'd sucked his balls dry by the time the seat-belt sign came off.'

I winced at his choice of words. 'I don't believe a word you say, Seth. After all, Mr Mistry is such a distinguished diplomat, he would have searched high and low for a suitable companion.'

'Poor misguided Naidu! He's a diplomat all right, but only cosmetically, you understand. The fellow happens to be obscenely loaded. Damn convenient at

84

election time, so they let him play at being the grand old man of diplomacy. Anyway, why am I telling you all this?'

'What do you mean, loaded? He comes from an old, established Lucknow family, doesn't he?' I looked at Seth in alarm. This was treachery.

That snort again. 'Yes, and I'm J. F. Kennedy! What a damn good double-act they make. She spreads open her legs and he flicks open his cheque-book. Oh, just look at that hurt face.' Leaning forward, Seth mockingly raised my chin. 'Those Kathakali eyes again, and that Mills and Boon heart. Don't tell me you've fallen for her? So much for the devoted *desi* husband.' Another drag at his cigarette and Seth continued with his attack. 'The itch in the pants – never thought it could affect a simpleton like you. Keep away from her, Naidu, keep away, I'm warning you. Much as I'd relish the spectacle of that tigress mauling you, against my better judgment I'm warning you.'

The insolence of the man! He was misreading me again. But how could I tell him that it was I who was being pursued? I had done my level best to remain faithful.

Was this the secret behind Mrs Mistry's mysterious attraction to me? Had I been chosen for purely carnal reasons? Somehow, it did not ring true. Call it what you will, sixth sense or a poet's intuition, someone of Mrs Mistry's pedigree could hardly be said to be behaving like a harlot. She was a lady right down to her toetips, even though in private she was carried away. This was nothing but envy. Seth, aware of her love interest in me, had no doubt been smarting ever since and used these insulting tactics to soothe his own ego.

'I think we've exchanged enough confidences to last a lifetime. I must rush now. The train for Oxford leaves in half an hour.' Seth peered at his watch, an expensive glint of metal and gold. 'I might just catch it if I'm lucky.'

How long I remained on that bench I do not remember. The stars above me were like Diwali lamps hung out of reach. Now and then a passer-by taking a short-cut through the park would look at me and quicken his step. My heart and mind were locked in a confusing battle of will. On one hand lay the memory of my family and duties shrugged carelessly aside, on the other lay the image of Naina's predatory passion.

CHAPTER THIRTEEN

A lunch is thrown

⌐⌐

The tinkle of glass,
the glow of candlelight,
the whisper of loving friends.
Can my heart be blamed
if it swells in delight?

(Excerpt from a work in progress)

NAINA HAD NOT promised in vain. With determined
efficiency, she set about collecting what she described
as the most photogenic names and faces to grace her
luncheon table. The promptness of their acceptance
surprised me, but then, as Naina wisely observed after
yet another hectic amorous encounter, the English will
murder their grannies for a free meal with a blue-
blooded memsahib.

There it lay, the actual invitation, in gold letters
against creamy white: '*Her Excellency Madame Naina*
Mistry seeks the pleasure of your company at a lunch to
celebrate the arrival in England of Mr Kavi Naidu, Poet and
distinguished Man of Letters.'

Grateful tears flooded my eyes. Such blind faith, and
she had yet to read a single word written by me.

This last fact rankled slightly. Time and again I had tried to persuade Mrs Mistry to read my manuscript, but with no success. Each time, accompanied by the same throaty laugh, her hand would reach out and speculatively wander down my belly. 'My Nadino, your other modest talents will have to do for now.' In sheer frustration, I had sneaked a copy of my love poems into her bathroom. At least there, in her moments of idleness, she could soak in a couplet or two. But not a single reference to the work had been forthcoming.

Naina's instructions came back to me as I squeezed the last of Shivaji's Gentleman pomade onto my hair: 'You must look like an authentic *desi* son of the soil. I will not have you looking like a half-baked Brindian in a shiny suit.'

'Brindian', as she patiently explained to me, referred to those who swung helplessly between being neither fully British nor fully Indian. England was overflowing with specimens of this kind, so Naina informed me. Personally, I found the predicament to warrant sympathy rather than insult. Rather romantically, I thought of these Brindians as exiles with no kingdom to reclaim. Naina, however, was less forgiving: 'Mongrels with two masters to bite. I wouldn't trust them for a minute.'

In deference to her wishes, I reluctantly wore the khaki Nehru jacket. It did little justice to my waistline, but I must not look 'Brindian', so the dashing Savile Row-style suit remained folded in the suitcase. Clutching my *Shipwrecked Tears*, I set out for the restaurant, surprisingly calm for such a momentous event. Seth's absence was the main reason for my composure; there was no fear of being eclipsed. The cream of English society, an attentive Mrs Mistry, good food and wine (under her tutelage, I had reluctantly taken to imbibing a sip or two of that inebriating elixir): what more could a poet on the brink of stardom want?

I almost missed the restaurant, tucked away as it was in a narrow side street. Where was the sweeping drive, the five-star lobby, the turbaned guard springing to open the heavy glass door? The walls of Chez Gerard were bare except for a large painting of a reclining lady dressed in nothing but a necklace. I had imagined something entirely different: a huge marble floor, crystal chandeliers from Bohemia and feet sinking into Persian rugs. If this was where the glitterati of London entertained, we Delhiites could easily teach them a thing or two. I looked at Naina doubtfully as we made our way across a bare wooden floor. Was this promotion being done on the cheap? Even Billo's was deluxe in comparison.

The hand-picked guests were already there, six in all, and all rose to their feet on seeing Naina, such was her imperial presence. Indeed, one elderly gentleman with bright peacock-blue eyes and a pink-freckled bird-like neck was so bold as to take her hand and kiss it thrice. There was much cheek kissing and shaking of hands and suddenly we were all seated. Much to my chagrin, Naina had seated herself at the furthest end from me. I was stuck between the owner of the freckled neck and a hippie-type gentleman wearing a violent orange tie. His greasy ponytail brushed against my shoulder every time he nodded.

As agreed beforehand, I took Naina's lead in ordering the food. 'Same as Madam, please,' I repeated dutifully each time the sulky waiter looked vaguely in my direction. I just hoped she had remembered I was strictly Indian vegetarian on account of an upset tummy. English food, with its subtle seasonings, unfortunately did not seem to agree with my digestive system. There was much heated debate and time wasting among the others concerning the nationality and colour of wines to be consumed. In the end, a theatrical gentleman wearing a garland of medals was summoned to make up their minds.

Once the solemn business of ordering was over, the conversation burst around me like the peel of an over-ripe fruit. They all knew each other well. My Nehru collar felt hot and tight as appraising eyes looked at me expectantly. Apart from me, there was one other Indian gentleman, a sculptor with a Dr Zhivago-style of looks who specialised in casting the hands of middle-aged women in bronze. After giving me a quick, searching glance, he ignored me politely for the rest of the meal, concentrating instead on lavishing compliment upon compliment on Naina, who played along cheerfully.

So swift and competent was she with her introductions that I could not register a single name and made a mental note to enquire later. All I could catch was that I was sitting in the company of two titled lords, one of them the owner of a publishing house, a high-ranking civil servant from the British Council, the CEO of a large European publishing company and the chief editor of a fashion magazine.

The owner of the freckled neck turned to me. 'And what kind of publications have you been associated with, Mr Naidu? I confess I have not had the pleasure of encountering your work before.' He had a thin wavering voice which sank to a whisper at the end of each sentence. The others leaned forward and smiled encouragingly.

I smiled back, but before I could speak Naina interceded on my behalf. 'Do speak slowly, Weinberg, or Naidu might have trouble following. He's spent most of his life in Proustian soul-searching. You know: reclusive, withdrawn genius, that sort of thing. His talent was discovered quite by accident, only recently, by none other than our good friend Seth.'

I looked at her in astonishment. Why on earth was she describing me as some ash-smeared invalid guru rescued by Seth? But before I could defend my reputation, the first course arrived: a giant cockroach-like insect, lying on its back and swimming in a creamy green sauce, stared reproachfully at me.

'Lobster thermidor,' announced the waiter proudly.

A reverential silence fell upon the table as everybody attacked the pink carcasses swimming in their respective plates. I watched in fascination as Naina deftly broke open a claw and sucked the juice with visible satisfaction. Miserably I toyed with my spoon and in a moment of bravery scooped up some of the green juice.

The waiter was clearing the plates when I returned from the bathroom after spitting out that vile stuff. The remaining courses simply continued the parade of lifelike dead flesh. The sauces dressing them cried out for chillies and garam masala. And this was meant to be the crowning jewel of London dining!

All around me was the sound of breaking bones and of knives being scratched against delicate cream-coloured plates. I watched the proceedings with a detached, superior, Kamala-the-vegetarian smile. (This smile greeted us at home whenever Amma defiantly prepared butter chicken on the last Sunday of every month.) Silently I helped myself to two rolls of bread lying forgotten behind the vase of orchids.

Greasy ponytail, seeing the carcass lying unmolested on my plate, considerately offered me some of his leftover salad. 'But you gurus are probably more used to feasting on thin air.' He laughed uproariously.

The moment was right to clear up any delusions regarding my saintly status.

'Actually, I am no guru-vuru, Mister. I happen to be a senior government official with a published track record. I have always enjoyed robust health in the modern city of Delhi, and have been a poet, by the grace of God, for some fifteen years now – in English, too, which I regard as my mother tongue, really.' I looked around triumphantly and placed the copy of *Shipwrecked Tears* right in the centre of the table. I had succeeded in holding their attention. Hands paused in mid-air and eyebrows were raised at this frank admission.

Pleased at the response, I turned to the British Council official, who was rubbing away at his mouth with a napkin. 'Indeed, it is your illustrious institution I must thank for stirring the first sparks of poetry.' I then proceeded to tell them about the significance of those boyhood trips to the library. There were several oohs and aahs of approval, and Naina suddenly excused herself and made for the toilets. The Indian sculptor, obviously cut up by the attention being showered on me, began picking his teeth and staring at me in a most insolent fashion.

By some devilish design, the conversation soon turned to Seth. The European publisher, in particular, was keen to know whether I shared his interest in metaphysics and whether a collaboration was forthcoming.

'My dear friend,' I replied in a louder voice than usual, for the benefit of Naina, who had returned but had gone all quiet, 'Seth and I are as chalk to cheese. He is the surgeon of the skull, while my expertise is the beating heart. If you will permit me . . .' I glanced through my book and picked out a verse at random.

> 'The heart when it holds the pen
> to write the beloved's name
> is mightier than a Herculean sword
> Clashing on a battlefield.'

The titled lords greeted the recitation with generous bravos, but the others were less forthcoming. Typical Anglo-Saxon reserve, I suppose. Naina wore an extremely animated look and plunged immediately into an outrageously amusing anecdote about the time the Burmese Ambassador had lost his dentures inside her blouse.

From then on, the talk flowed on a lighter plane. I was advised about the various places for sightseeing and asked about my family. Questions were raised about Ravi Shankar and India's population policy. One gentleman wanted to know my opinion on the caste system. Luckily, Naina intervened and put him in his place with a few well-chosen remarks about the British class system. Every attempt to bring the talk back to poetry was firmly ignored by everyone.

Once or twice I tried to catch Naina's eye, to re-establish our solidarity, but she seemed determined to ignore my efforts, keeping her eyes firmly fixed on the vase of orchids in the middle of the table. Naturally, with her high profile, discretion was of paramount importance. Thankfully, the dessert arrived and I could hide my disappointment in a dark, rich chocolate cake. Why couldn't the others realise I was here to promote my poetry and sign publishing deals, not to discuss the best season for visiting the Taj Mahal?

The lunch, viewed from the launching angle, was a flop, even if socially I had made a mark. Indeed, Lord Weinberg was so kind as to invite me for some weekend shooting at his country house in the rainy northern state of Cheshire. Naina's mouth grew tighter and tighter as the meal drew to an end, and, increasingly reckless under the influence of wine, I replied to the most casual of questions only in rhyming couplets. After much air kissing and scraping of chairs, the guests vanished like a flock of crows chased away by a farmer. Not one photographer or journalist had materialised; not one autograph or follow-up talk on poetry had been solicited by those present.

Since I was furious with Mrs Mistry's amateur handling of the lunch, we drove back to the hotel in pin-drop silence.

'You do realise time is ticking by. How can I become a celebrity if no journalist is invited for me to be interviewed?' I finally rebuked Naina politely.

She hit back venomously. 'Why couldn't you keep your trap shut? There I was promoting you as a reclusive genius and all you could come up with was nursery-rhyme gibberish.'

Misery truly fell in bucketfuls that day. Once back in my room, I discovered to my horror that my cherished book had been left behind in that accursed restaurant, whose name I could not remember. There was divine retribution at work here. Kamala's gods were conspiring to ensure that I remained but an anonymous spark burning away in solitude. Just as I had reached this somewhat grim conclusion, a slim blue telegram was slipped beneath the door. I knew immediately who had sent it. It was Amma reclaiming her son.

'Anxiously awaiting competition outcome Stop Kamala determined to fast Stop Gupta restless in office Stop Feroze down with dysentery Stop Love Amma.'

How far away I stood from the daily trials and tribulations of Rouse Avenue.

CHAPTER FOURTEEN

An Englishman in his castle

VIEWED FROM A strictly literary angle, my lunch at Chez Gerard could be termed a flop, but the social fallout from it was far from negative. Invitations to attend art openings and literary discussions in such august institutions as the Institute of Education began to wing their way to the Modern Ascension Hotel. I had suddenly become a desirable social commodity. This public exposure could only enhance my chances of winning the prize.

'Be sure to recite at every available opportunity' was Amma's advice when I wrote to her describing the sudden surge in my popularity.

'I don't know which bloody mailing list you've got on to, but you seem to have wormed your way in well and good. How quick the damn English are to welcome waifs and strays under their roof,' Naina remarked uncharitably when I showed her the latest invitation. Abruptly I withdrew my hand, which she had somehow managed to insinuate into her blouse, and looked at her, hurt. Why did she insist on treating me like a literary impostor at times?

An invitation to spend the weekend at Lord Weinberg's country house in the rainy state of

Cheshire, or county as I was corrected on numerous subsequent occasions, was undoubtedly the crowning achievement of my visit to England.

'Lord Weinberg, no less . . . Hmm, he has the most envied wine cellar in the country. Lucky you to get an insight into how the upper crust lives here,' Mr Mistry murmured admiringly, running absent-minded fingers through his beard.

'Oh, I am well acquainted with the manners of the rich and famous here – after all, Jane Austen was a childhood heroine of mine.'

Any secret apprehension I might have felt at the thought of rubbing shoulders with blue-blooded English aristocracy vanished on learning that Naina had been invited in her own right. She would be an invaluable guide. As far as her amorous predilections were concerned, I would make sure the doors were bolted tight and secure against her knockings.

*

The rain-soaked English countryside sped past us as we left London. What was striking was the greenness of things and their size. Unlike in India, the trees, the grass, even the houses we passed, were of a manageable, good-natured size, designed for ease not obstruction. And how much preferable was the good-humoured pitter-patter of the rain here to the bone-dry heat of Delhi afternoons.

'But where is everybody?' I anxiously asked Naina. Miles and miles of countryside had passed without our encountering a single loitering person or animal.

'This isn't India, you know,' she replied crossly, 'where you can't even bloody breathe on your own. The

English are a very private people. They don't just barge out of their houses for nothing, every action has a purpose.'

*

Lord Weinberg's house, when it eventually swam into view through the thick cloud of drizzle, could hardly be termed a castle. The garden, unkempt and wild, had spread its green hairy fingers right up to the brickwork, which, sorely in need of a fresh coat of paint, gazed back at us, mournful and chipped. Oversized flowers, crudely coloured and resembling the private parts of humans, tumbled out of cracked marble urns. Several statues with various bits of their anatomy missing protruded at awkward angles from the roof. It reminded me in a curious way of Sharmila's *barsati* in Delhi – and this was the home of a man reputed to be one of the wealthiest in England!

'But what an utterly charming place!' Naina gushed in well-bred tones, emerging from the car. All trace of sleep had vanished from her eyes and, bending down from her majestic height, she smothered Lord Weinberg in a series of breathless, butterfly kisses. Gonzales, meanwhile, attentively waiting at the steering wheel, was shooed away with the most perfunctory of gestures.

'Naina, Naina, so glad you could make it along with your flying yogi.' Lord Weinberg beamed from top to toe. He was pinker than I remembered, and in the brisk outdoor air his cheeks shone like polished red apples from the Lajpat Nagar market. This gleam and sheen, I was sad to note, did not extend to his clothing, which looked extremely worn and old. He was wearing a faded raincoat-style military green jacket, a pair of mud-stained khaki trousers and ancient-looking boots; the top of one boot looked as though it had been bitten by an animal, possibly a rat. What an undignified way of receiving visitors, I thought, glancing down at my own three-piece suit.

Lady Weinberg soon joined us, tripping down the drive like an excited schoolgirl. Close on her heels were two enormous shaggy-haired dogs, which began barking joyfully on seeing us. With her rather large nose and prominent teeth, which she flashed at completely unexpected moments, she resembled Black Beauty. Her eyes, the colour of an overcast sky, lit up on seeing Naina.

'Dear, dear Naina, how terribly, terribly sweet of you to drop in on us.' This habit of saying things twice was one Lady Weinberg engaged in regularly, I soon found. 'And you, of course, of course.'

I was included in the welcome almost as an afterthought. Not that I minded. Everything was so new and exotic, I could not wait to plunge headlong into this authentic slice of English life.

The untidiness of the garden had spilled over into the house. Stacks of old newspapers, umbrellas, muddy hats and walking sticks obstructed our entry through the poorly lit hall. Lady Weinberg, I was shocked to notice, thought nothing of this disarray and, far from apologising profusely, insisted on highlighting aspects of the shabbiness to Naina.

'That is Richard's great-aunt, Naina. You know, the one who was Edward's mistress. Isn't she an absolute, absolute wreck, darling?'

I looked carefully at the huge painting tilting dangerously on the wall. A large woman with an elaborate hairstyle and the same striking nose as Lord Weinberg looked down aristocratically at us through a thin film of dust. I glanced at Naina to see how she, with her refined taste in Italian marble and Chinese silks, would take to this squalor. But Naina was gushing away delightedly, pressing Lady Weinberg's hand in a show of sisterly solidarity.

'What a miserable cow she looks, Annabel, and to think she almost brought down the throne. Ridiculous, no?'

We were led not into the drawing room, as I had imagined, but into the kitchen, where a large fire threw intermittent angry shadows through the room. A wooden table covered in breadcrumbs and several cups of half-finished tea stood in the centre. Above it dangled a collection of rusty pots and pans, hung from enormous hooks jutting from the wooden ceiling.

'Just like a medieval kitchen,' I observed knowledgeably to Naina, who chose to ignore my remark.

The two dogs, which had not left our side, made straight for a spot in front of the fireplace and flopped down, eyes glazed, tongues lolling out.

'Oh, the poor dears, the poor dears, absolutely flaked out. Richard, did you take Percy and Galahad for a run this morning?' Lady Weinberg's watery grey eyes narrowed accusingly.

What a considerate mother yet what an ill-tempered wife she was.

'And how old are the children, Lady Weinberg?' I imagined their two sons, Percy and Galahad, to be down for the weekend from Oxford, still idling in bed.

This innocent query had a dramatic effect on Lady Weinberg, who, with an animal-sounding howl, her mouth going all lopsided and weak, collapsed onto a sagging sofa covered in biscuit crumbs and burst into a storm of tears.

'I knew Richard did the right thing in inviting you, a holy yogi, over. Tell me how did you, how did you know?' My hands were seized and her hot, fleshy lips pressed down on them. 'I know you'll be able to help me, help me.' Beseeching eyes looked up at me.

Lord Weinberg had meanwhile appeared with a glass of some dark beverage and he began pressing it upon his wife. 'Down it in one gulp, Annabel. Steady now, steady,' he whispered, patting her shoulder comfortingly.

'You ignorant oaf!' Naina hissed angrily into my ear. 'In less than ten minutes you have succeeded in upsetting our hosts and ruining the entire weekend.' Then she turned to Annabel and said cheerfully, 'Now you just take it easy, dearie. We'll see our own way upstairs. The West Wing, isn't it?'

Bewildered, I followed Naina meekly up the dimly lit stairs. What social blunder had I unknowingly committed? In my place, Seth would undoubtedly have known the answers.

Naina brusquely showed me into a small, dark room which went by the romantic French name of *chambre de bonne*. The narrow, stained window looked down upon miles and miles of unblinking green countryside. A solitary crow sat guarding an electric pylon, and far in the distance I could see rain-bearing clouds rolling determinedly towards us. A sudden feeling of sadness seized me. What was I doing in this house full of foreigners?

There is darkness drifting around,
Clouds heavy with rain.

Is it their wetness I feel upon my cheek?
Or is it liquid of another sadder kind?

'Naina?' We had been intimate in so many ways, yet a certain fear still caught me whenever I had to use her name. 'Did I do something wrong?'

'Something wrong! Only the social *faux pas* of the century. Don't you know the Weinbergs lost their two sons some years back? Car accident in Monte Carlo, I think it was. And then you had to go and bring children up. Remember, Naidu, if you are to mingle successfully in these circles, keep your talk limited to sex, dogs and the monarchy.' And with these cutting words, she left the room.

Hoping to make amends to my hosts, I decided to go down. I found Lady Weinberg, now in a much calmer frame of mind, giving her two dogs a vigorous bath in the kitchen while singing a Scottish lullaby. Tendrils of rough brown hair escaped from the silk scarf she had tied loosely around her head. The two dogs lay, heads nestled in her lap, soft fur smothered in lather, trusting eyes gazing heavenward.

'Man's best friend, eh?' I said, kneeling down and pulling one canine ear affectionately. 'I am sorry I upset you earlier, Lady Weinberg – it was not my intention. As a poet, you see, I am usually highly tuned to human suffering.'

Lady Weinberg looked at me with watery eyes, and her large mouth with its row of uneven yellow teeth broke into a forgiving smile. 'Don't worry about that. Happens to me all the time, all the time. Still haven't got used to it. Richard tells me you're a mystic, years spent fasting in a jungle . . . I knew it, that aura above your head. You are here to help.' Leaving her scrubbing, she gazed dreamily into the distance.

It could only be Naina spreading this web of malicious misinformation. Why on earth did she not wish me to be known by my true calling? Before I could refute this unjustified attribution, some unexpected visitors arrived. It was none other than Seth, accompanied by the mocking sculptor from my lunch at Chez Gerard.

'Visitors! More visitors. Don't mind me. Don't I love it when he collects you all to come calling all the way from London town? What a rip-roaring, rip-roaring weekend we shall, we shall have,' Lady Weinberg shrieked excitedly, rocking on her heels. Soapsuds from her vigorous bathing exercise flew into her eyes, from which a steady stream of water began to trickle.

Callously ignoring this effusive greeting, Seth and the sculptor stepped past the messy puddle on the floor and Seth shouted, 'Weinberg, where are you?' More quietly, he asked, 'Where's the old man, Annabel? He promised us a bit of shooting.' Then another shout: 'Weinberg, where the devil are you? The VIPs are here.'

I was most annoyed by Seth's arrival. The whole tone of the weekend would now change, all cutting remarks and innuendoes, and I would be forced to compete for the same adoring audience.

'Look, Mr Nuisance is here as well.' Seth had at last caught sight of me. 'You're just like a boomerang, Naidu – no matter how far one throws you, you always come whining back for more.' Laughing at his own display of wit, he called, 'Weinberg, face up to your duties, man. We demand to be entertained.'

Seth, I was quick to note, seemed very much at ease in these English surroundings. Dressed in the same sort of faded corduroys as his host, he had placed a green military-style beret on his head, which gave his face a roguish look. His companion, the quiet Dr Zhivago-lookalike sculptor, dressed in similar fashion, was in addition puffing away at a cigar, amused brown eyes looking through me all the while.

Lord Weinberg came in and exchanged greetings with the newcomers.

He glanced over at me. 'Joining us? Or do you prefer the company of petticoats?' he asked over his shoulder, pulling two ominous-looking rifles from a cabinet. Tempted as I was to decline his offer and stay with his wife, drinking cups of tea and listening to her unburden her soul, something in the demeanour of the other two men made me change my mind. Why should they be alone in sampling a slice of genuine English life?

The sky seemed lower than before as we set off, trudging across dirty, muddy fields into which my Delhi soft shoes sank uncomfortably. A light rain began tip-tapping against my double-breasted suit, which was proving hopelessly inadequate in the face of this inclement weather. I looked enviously at Seth and his friend, who were striding ahead in their sturdy footwear and warm green jackets. Why had nobody bothered to inform me that it was usual to dress badly but warmly in top-class English families?

Once or twice Lord Weinberg threw me an almost pitying glance. 'Sure you can manage this?' he asked doubtfully. 'Don't want you passing out on us.'

At last, we stood in a muddy green patch bordered by a low wooden fence. The patch stretched as far as the eye could see, with little clusters of sheep and cows now and then breaking up the green monotony.

'How one misses the daffodils of Wordsworth,' I said by way of conversation to Seth and his bearded companion.

'Wrong season, old chap,' Seth remarked curtly, and he sauntered off to join Weinberg, who was engaged in fierce discussion with a short, pockmarked peasant carrying a rough khaki sack.

We were directed to a clear, raised spot in the middle of the field and then suddenly, without warning, a lump of clay was catapulted by the peasant into the air, as he quickly ducked behind a small, makeshift wooden partition. Lord Weinberg stepped back, squinted his eye, gazed in rapt concentration at the falling clod, raised the rifle and fired. He missed all three pulls, and with a sulky growl handed over the gun to Seth, who made a great show of arranging his limbs in a suitably military pose. Much to my delight, he also missed the falling missiles.

'Too much champagne last night' was the feeble excuse he offered, before boasting about his shooting prowess at Oxford.

The whole exercise was beginning to seem ultra-childish. Why not use real, live pigeons? After all, we were all grown men.

My suggestion seemed to shock Weinberg, who threw up his hands in horror. 'What kind of barbaric talk is this? We respect life in these parts, you know.'

Suitably chastened, I quietly awaited instructions with a pounding heart. Being the cerebral kind, I had no illusions about my sporting skills. Soon it was my turn to take aim, the sculptor having declined on aesthetic grounds. Some dirty foam was roughly pushed into my ears by the swarthy farmer, whose dialect I failed to understand. Contrary to all the advice shouted in my direction, I obstinately closed both eyes and briefly thought of Kamala and her pantheon of gods. My shoulder almost sank under the weight of the gun as I gently pulled the trigger. Whether by fluke or force of destiny, the bullet found its target each time. With a soft sigh, the pieces of mud disintegrated in the air in rapid succession. I looked around in triumph as the coarse farmer ran up to me and thumped my back in an over-familiar manner.

'A natural-born Rambo,' he proudly announced to the assembled company.

I was the uncrowned hero of the afternoon. Not for me the lame excuses of Seth's so-called slipped disc or Lord Weinberg's plea of gout. Either one was a natural marksman or one was not. I fleetingly contemplated a career in the armed forces, as Lord Weinberg forcibly emptied a little silver flask into my mouth.

'Quick,' he ordered, 'down the hatch. You're trembling like a lily-livered virgin.'

*

In an attempt to blend in with the informal surroundings, I opted for rather casual trousers and checked bush-shirt for dinner. My suit was anyway far too mud-splattered to be of use. Imagine my surprise, then, on seeing the entire company dressed formally in black from head to toe.

Lady Weinberg was transformed by the glow of candlelight. Her pale, rather broad shoulders gleamed healthily through her transparent gown, and a long rope of pearls hung from her neck. Noticing me lingering rather timidly by the drawing-room door, she immediately led me to the most comfortable seat near the fireplace.

The room was very dark. How frugal the English upper classes were, saving electricity even when entertaining. The mantelpiece directly behind me was the only impressive feature in the room, crowded as it was with ornate bric-a-brac and a drooping bouquet of dried flowers. I firmly refused the drink Lady Weinberg tried to press upon me, as my head was still spinning from the contents of that silver flask.

'Of course, how ignorant of me,' she apologised. 'You mystics don't touch anything but water.'

I looked around for Naina, and found her holding court in the darkest corner of the room. The bearded sculptor with the light brown eyes stood uncomfortably close to her, while Seth was busy pontificating, scissoring the air with his long, well-manicured fingers.

'So, tell me, is there hope of my conceiving again, even at my age, my age?' Lady Weinberg asked me in an anxious whisper, lower lip wavering ever so slightly.

So earnest did she look that I did not have the heart to disappoint her. I nodded. 'Yes, there are ways. Maybe the solution can be fasting or some special prayer.' I quoted her one of Kamala's favourite lines: 'God has many ways, and one of them is destined for you.' Before I could be probed any further, I quickly made for Naina.

'Aha, Naidu, our man for all seasons,' she remarked, 'absolutely without reason. Just where do you think you might be heading in that safari shirt? Though, judging by the rumours I've heard, you were quite a shooting star this afternoon,' and she tweaked my collar affectionately.

I glowed at the compliment, forgetting for an instant that it was my molester uttering them. The sculptor, made insecure, no doubt, by this sudden shift of Naina's attention, pounced on me.

'Naina, I just had this wonderful idea. We have two poets here, one a poet's poet, the other' – he looked scornfully at me – 'still struggling to make two rhymes meet, so why not have a sort of verbal duel between them after dinner? A fist-fight with words. It would make a change from dumb charades or Scrabble, *n'est ce pas?*' The show-off actually finished in French.

His light brown eyes were glowing and the cleft in his chin became deeper as he spoke. I remembered Amma's warning to Kamala: 'Beware the company of a cleft-chinned man. They are born scoundrels, born stealers of hearts.'

'Oh, no, we couldn't do that to Naidino,' said Naina in a lazy drawl. 'He wouldn't last a moment.'

Leaning forward, she unceremoniously snatched the cigarette from Seth's mouth. The candlelight caught the nape of her neck where a solitary tendril of hair floated dreamily. Her long, bare arms casually brushed against my side. What kind of daredevil game was she playing?

'On the contrary, I will be most delighted to pit my modest talents against Seth Sahib.' I hoped I sounded confident enough. Seth with his oratorical skills would reduce me to pulp in no time, but I was not prepared to go down without a fight.

I do not remember much of the dinner, preoccupied as I was with thoughts of the coming duel. All I recall is a large, shadowy hall and an immense table covered with a bewildering array of glasses. Two smartly dressed servants materialised out of nowhere and silently helped us through a succession of dishes, each course blander than the one before.

Lady Weinberg, noticing me shiver, thoughtfully draped her lace shawl round me. 'Poor, poor man. How terribly, terribly alien it must seem . . . all this cutlery. I bet you're pining for your Himalayan cave and a bowl of Ganges water.'

Seth, at the other end of the table, was regaling the rest with an amusing escapade from his Oxford days. Lord Weinberg was almost falling off his chair with laughter, while the sculptor was examining Naina's hands in a very urgent, intense way.

A platter of smelly cheese concluded a thoroughly inadequate meal, even though I was the first to praise it sky-high to Lady Weinberg, who murmured as if to herself, 'It's nothing, nothing. Just Agatha, our cook from Germany. She does all these wonderful things with potatoes, wonderful things. But I really should be fasting, you said? Or feasting?'

We reassembled in the drawing room, where further drinks and cigars were provided. The ladies suddenly vanished, 'to powder their noses', Lord Weinberg informed me, swaying unsteadily on his feet. The lower two buttons of his tight-fitting jacket had been opened, and his trouser belt, unfastened, dangled in the air.

'Are you all right, sir? If you want we can all leave now and you can have some sleep,' I offered.

'Sleep?' Lord Weinberg spat out the word in contempt. 'Sleep is death all dressed up with nowhere to go. The hell I want to sleep! Some more port, gentlemen?' And going over to Seth, he poured another round of drinks.

What an obscene amount the English drank. All this tea drinking was a façade. Deep down they were all Scotch whisky-lovers, each and every one of them. Lost as I was in these jingoistic observations, I failed to notice the reappearance of the ladies, who were sparkling even more than before.

Naina clapped her hands authoritatively. 'Wakey, wakey, all of you. Stop looking like grazing goats in purgatory. Naidu, ready for some sparring?'

Seth decided to play coy and reluctant. 'Oh, such a bore. Have pity on the poor sod.'

'No, no, no. Let the games begin and let the subject be love. Love eternal,' Lady Weinberg piped up from the floor where she sat hiding her face in the woolly warmth of her two dogs, one of which was licking her pearls greedily, his pink tongue darting in and out. The other, head burrowed in her lap, gnawed away quietly at the lace trimming of her dress. How intimate English animals were with their owners.

'Love? That happens to be my speciality.' I immediately felt confident and, clearing my throat, began without further prompting.

> 'The fragile flutter of lashes upon your cheek.
> The dark, stormy cloud of your hair upon my
>   shoulder.
> Your words softly promising me undying love.'

Emotion prevented me from speaking further. Lady Weinberg clapped and, raising her glass, loudly cried, 'Bravo! Bravo, Shelley!'

Her husband, now almost horizontal on the sofa, silenced her with a 'Shush, woman, you're destroying Seth's concentration.'

Instead of Seth, it was the sculptor who spoke. Seth had whispered something in his ear and now, boldly taking Naina's hand, he recited these words:

> 'I want love.
> Gut-wrenching
> Lip-bleeding
> Mind-churning
> Palm-sweating
> Night-waking Love.'

Naina sighed dramatically on hearing it and loosened her hair. It fell like a cascade of steps upon her shoulder.

'He hasn't finished,' Seth said crossly, and took over in a loud, booming voice.

> 'I want love.
> Not this pale breathing of
> Polite, timid words.
> Well-mannered mumbled Thank-Yous in the
>   dark.
> The dimming of lights within, without.'

A reverential hush fell. Lord Weinberg sat up abruptly in his chair, mouth open in wonder. Lady Weinberg, her head pressed against the shaggy, furry stomach of her dogs, let out a long squeal of delight.

'Ooooh, that made the hairs on my neck stand up,' gushed Naina, going over to Seth and giving him a bold kiss on the lips.

It was time to retaliate.

> 'There is Love built on the desire of flesh.
> The mating of bodies in the darkening night.

Then there is my love,
A meeting of pure minds.'

But there was no enthusiastic reaction.

'Derivative crap as usual,' muttered Seth, picking up his jacket, which he had flung aside casually. He raised one hand in farewell and made nonchalantly for the door.

'Are you letting Naidu have the last word?' Naina teased him, leaning provocatively against the door. The light from the corridor behind lit up her dress, making it diaphanous so that the outline of her shapely limbs could be seen by all.

'I bow before such loveliness.' Seth gave a mock bow and raised her fingers to his lips. 'This, Naina, could almost have been written for you:

'Let me scratch your skin to see
Where yours begins and mine ends.
This biting of mouths. Your upturned face,
The lips held so slightly apart.
The way your hands spread over my back.
The tensing of each muscle, the closing of eye.
Let me carry these like trophies, to decorate
The darkness that surely must lie ahead.'

'Thoroughly X-rated stuff. Thoroughly to my liking,' said Naina, giving a cat-like stretch and abruptly leaving us with a quick 'good night'.

Seth and the sculptor exchanged a cryptic smile before following her out of the room. I smiled in relief; at least tonight my limbs were free from molestation. Even so, I would make sure I double-locked my door.

*

112

Lady Weinberg waylaid me the next morning, as I was polishing my shoes. Dressed again in her manly, shabby clothes, she seemed very different from the pearl-wearing lady of the previous night.

'I can't let you leave without giving me the potion.'

I looked at her blankly and then suddenly remembered. The poor woman wanted to bear children again.

'Actually, it isn't medicine I am prescribing, just some simple words. Being a poet, that is the only medicine I can give. Please recite these nightly before going to sleep.'

Lady Weinberg nodded like an obedient student, and carefully copied out the following words in an old notebook.

> *'The cooing of babies, the feel of soft hands.*
> *Tiny arms clasped tight around my chest.*
> *Dear God, let me feel once more,*
> *The beating of a mother's breast.'*

'What strange sorts these English upper classes are . . . like coconuts with their soft insides. All this feeling swirling within. This visit has been most educational,' I remarked to Naina, on our way back to London.

'No need to get so misty-eyed about that worthless lot. And what English? He's a bloody second-generation Sephardic Jew, and her father started out at a lacemaking factory in Liverpool. They kid nobody with those posh accents of theirs.'

What a ruthless way Naina had of cutting people down to size.

CHAPTER FIFTEEN

Judgement day

∽

I HAD A dream. I was riding a horse round the Colosseum in a curious re-run from some old American film, the sort one skipped the Sanskrit class in school to watch during those unbearably hot Delhi afternoons. The set was pure *Ben-Hur*, the same crayon-blue sky in the distance. I could make out Mr Mistry's toga-clothed body, gleaming against a bronze throne. At his feet lay two familiar figures, Naina and, surprise, surprise, Mrs Pereira. Wearing brilliant technicolored bikinis, they looked like mythical creatures symbolising day and night, Mrs Pereira's glossy *brinjal* darkness a perfect foil to Naina's magnolia-petal paleness.

The horse I was riding neighed restlessly but I could not tear my eyes away from the two women, who were intently feeding Mistry succulent grapes and figs. With one hand, he caressed his goatee beard, while the other made urgent explorations of Mrs Pereira's bare midriff. And Naina? The panting, moist belly of my horse dissolved and it was Naina I was riding, her shrill cries growing louder and louder as my thighs dug deeper into her. Her hair was an unruly nest of curls entangling my limbs, her mouth open wide, ruby-red with desire. I thrust deeper and deeper into her.

*

Ashamed, I woke up soaked to the skin. Even my dreams had become polluted under English skies. It was the day of the prize-giving. Outside my hotel window, the morning lay limp and grey like one of Mrs Pereira's overwashed bedspreads. Far in the distance, I could hear the urgent wailing of a police siren and the screeching of tyres rushing out of reach. My whole life had been racing up to this moment, a kind of dress rehearsal, if you like, for this most prestigious of prizes, and here I lay, limbs still numb from the after-effects of my technicolored dream, reflecting glumly on the unremarkable noises of a remarkable day. I longed above all for Amma's comforting hand.

The omens were far from good. After the weekend at Lord Weinberg's, Naina had thankfully gone into temporary carnal hibernation and I had spent a restful day or two flicking through back issues of *Goa Today* in the hotel lobby and staring at the two life-size posters of Mother Teresa and Mohammed Ali that now dominated the walls. When questioned, Mrs Pereira claimed the images represented the twin facets of human nature: strength and kindness.

How would Seth be reacting to the dawning of this significant day? In fact, where was he? Busy sniffing out some new self-advancement opportunity, no doubt.

The actual prize-giving ceremony was not till late evening, and on impulse I decided to visit Mr Mistry for some last-minute fatherly advice and encouragement. As I made my way to his residence, little details stood out like an ominous leitmotif for the day. For instance, when I reached the corner of Charing Cross Road, right past the newsagent where the friendly Gujerati lady greeted me every morning with the same cheerful '*Kavi bhai, kemcho*', an English tramp waylaid me and demanded to know, as one brother to another, my views on the state of the trade unions in Her Majesty's land, and in particular about some Scarecrow chap. This spirit of civilised enquiry was so typical of the English. I mean, how many of our beggars would express or seek an opinion on the corruption in the Indian Civil Service or Jagjivan Ram? With them, it was always the same old selfish cry of empty bellies and hungry mouths.

Regretfully I informed the tramp of my ignorance of English current affairs. But he held on to my sleeve and started shaking it in a most persistent fashion, his breath forming little angry bubbles in the cool morning air. I could detect the smell of alcohol. 'Poetry Prize Recipient Stabbed to Death by London Tramp': I could see the screaming headlines in the *Hindustan Times*. Anxious to avoid such an inauspicious end, I made for the nearest escape, the underground station.

This underworld, which I was sampling for the first time, had a life of its own. All around me, men and women marched with grim determination, the sickly striplights overhead bleeding their faces to a sinister pallor. Cigarette stubs, old newspapers, mucus-soaked tissue, even a vaccination syringe or two, lay at my feet. And these foreigners complained that India was dirty! How much healthier seemed the grimy, noisy openness of our humble DTC buses back home.

I wanted directions, but from whom? All eyes were focused downwards, mouths buttoned tight, hands clutched earthly possessions – a briefcase, a newspaper. The women walked in tight little steps, busy eyes darting here and there, and not one had the civility to stop and answer my enquiry as to how I could get to number one Park Crescent.

I had seen the decline and fall of the West. The Age of Kaliyug was right here on this platform, spelled out on that public-health poster recommending universal condom usage for the teenage population of Britain. Just the thought of Feroze engaging in premarital intercourse, and that in his tender teen years and with the benign blessings of the state, was enough to make me nauseous. It was time to go home. I would simply collect my prize and catch the next flight back. Feroze needed an upstanding father's guiding moral hand.

I don't know how long I stood there lost in these thoughts, but eventually a thickset Sikh gentleman sweeping the floor with vigorous *bhangra*-type movements took pity on my plight and came over. The blue badge on his left pocket proclaimed him to be an employee of London Transport. Acknowledging me as a fellow countryman, he addressed me in friendly Jullandari Punjabi. I listened politely to his instructions about changing from the Circle line to the District at some place called the Liverpool Station, which was in fact in London, and the moment his back was turned made a rapid about-turn for the exit.

*

The Mistrys' drawing room looked restful in the late afternoon light. The smell of freshly mown grass filtered into the room through the open windows. A quiet, diminutive domestic was zealously polishing the chandeliers, perched on top of a ladder like a stranded sparrow. Giving him a dignified nod, I made for the alcove where I had first been manhandled by Naina.

Mr Mistry was seated there, exuding a Buddha-like serenity.

'Sir, what a surprise! I had not expected to find you here,' I exclaimed in confusion.

'Not expected me in my own home?' Mr Mistry gave me an amused smile and bade me sit down. Taking a magnifying glass from his pocket, he resumed his perusal of some thin, parchment-yellow papers which looked like maps. What top-level diplomatic research had I interrupted?

'Persia in the eighteenth century, a passion since childhood.' Mr Mistry broke the awkward silence with these mysterious words, and rolled up the onion-skin paper carefully.

No question about it, he intrigued me. I could not work out his relationship with Naina, that she could openly engage in riotous love with another man and he remained oblivious. This two and two definitely did not make four. The only way I could ease my conscience in all this was to assume that Mr Mistry enjoyed some kind of enlightened Marxist delight in sharing the temptations of the female flesh.

His next question added to my discomfiture. 'You will be looking for Naina, no doubt? I don't know where she is, though I suspect Father O'Brian may have a better idea.'

I must have looked surprised, for he continued with a laugh, 'Panic not, Naidu. She hasn't retreated to a convent. Father O'Brian runs a centre for abused women in Manchester and is doing the usual fundraising rounds. And Naina, not surprisingly, has embraced his cause.'

'But what about the prize-giving today? Surely, sir, shouldn't that be requiring your full-scale commitment?' Hurt, regret, disappointment, every adjective covering these emotions must have entered my voice for he looked at me pityingly.

'Pure as the first fall of snow in Simla, that's how you are, my dear Naidu. When you reach my stature you will realise these occasions are simply photo-grabbing excuses. Unlike me, Naina is like the multi-armed Durga: no cause is too small, no subject too unworthy, for her divine intervention. Especially' – he paused, and his eyes sparkled for an instant – 'where compassionate pursuits are concerned.'

Was this an indirect stab aimed at my status as Naina's unwilling paramour? I was tempted there and then to confess all. To lay down the humiliating facts about my seduction for him to judge. Being such a cerebral man, Mr Mistry would find the strength to forgive and forget. But, intellect or no intellect, would he emotionally be able to bear such a painful revelation? I was saved from any such disclosures by the arrival of the guilty party herself.

Her beauty like a marble bust of Ancient Greece.
There is softness in her eyes and fire in her womb.

Those words written long ago when I was a precocious twenty-year-old aptly captured the vision that entered the room. Naina floated in like fresh, blown spring air, holding an armful of roses. She had the clean, well-scrubbed look of a woman who has engaged in illicit sex in an uncomfortable hotel room. Her sari, a bright orange silk, was tied low round her waist, so low that her belly button gazed scornfully at the world and I could almost feel the tautness of her pelvic bones beneath the silk. I shifted uncomfortably in my seat.

Mr Mistry smiled at her indulgently, oblivious of the provocative mode of attire, ignoring the roses that screamed of betrayal, and pointed out the rolled maps to her. Was that man in need of glasses or simply too scholarly for his own good?

'How tired you look, *mon chéri*,' the temptress exclaimed, and, throwing aside the roses, she bent down and swiftly bit her husband's left earlobe, an endearment she had previously rehearsed on me. From the corner of my eye, I could see the Bihari domestic watching this show of marital affection with an open mouth.

Naina pressed a bell, and a second domestic appeared like a gunshot.

'Two gin and tonics, Ramu, and make that double quick, will you?' She had not yet spotted me.

'Those roses are beautiful, Madam, their colour complements your skin tone wonderfully.'

Naina swung round in surprise. Mr Mistry cleared his throat and started collecting his papers.

'What on bloody earth are you doing here, Naidu? Shouldn't you be worried sick about that damn prize-giving? The ceremony starts in an hour, you know.'

We could have been two passing ships in the night.

'Sorry for gatecrashing, Mrs Mistry, but I only came for a morale booster, a kind of pep talk from Mr Mistry to raise my spirits.'

'I see. Your spirits need raising, do they?' She looked at me mischievously. 'Let's see what we can do. Follow me to my study. Mistry, I won't be a moment.'

'No, no it's fine,' I entreated her, alarmed. 'I can be reassured right here in the open, no need for closed doors, just some . . . fatherly words.'

But my supplication fell on deaf ears.

'Go, Naidu, go. It will do you good. I'm hopeless at advising,' Mr Mistry said beatifically. 'By the way, Naina, was that O'Brian chap pestering you too much?' he continued absent-mindedly. The magnifying glass was out and the maps had been unrolled again.

'He was *so* persuasive. Such dedication and commitment to the cause. Why, I have a good mind to visit his centre in Manchester. You wouldn't mind, would you, darling?'

And, smiling sweetly, Naina led the way to her study just as a lamb is led to slaughter at Id.

As soon as the study door was slammed shut, Naina wrapped her arms around me

'My, I had forgotten how soft and podgy you are,' she murmured, one hand hurriedly opening the buttons of her blouse. Freed from the tight embrace of the silk blouse, Naina's breasts lay like low-slung fruit, heavy with promise.

My mouth was dry; I stood trembling and covered in sweat. The door of the study remained shut, but it might be opened at any instant by Mr Mistry.

I looked at the woman standing before me. 'Not today. Please do not attack me today. It is a sacred day, the day I come out of the wilderness.'

'Don't be such an absolute ass, Naidu. Tell me, it's a quickie you've come for, isn't it?'

'Naina!' I could not believe the crudeness of her words. 'It is a dialogue of souls I want, a reassurance that I will come out the winner.' Words were running away from me.

Giving an impatient laugh, Naina pushed me against the door. 'I'll tell you the sort of dialogue you want.'

Playfully, she patted my growing bump of manhood and savagely bit my left earlobe, an exact repetition of her actions a moment ago. Holding back my tears, I allowed her to unzip me and play with me as a baby would with a rattle.

CHAPTER SIXTEEN

Mrs Watanabe enters my life

〜

AN HOUR LATER, bruised and humiliated by the encounter with Naina, I found myself deposited on the steps of a building of excruciating ugliness. The Convention Centre, located in the religious heartland of London, next to Westminster Cathedral, resembled a body turned inside out, all functional pipes and tubes exposed on the outside, like intestines run amok. And this factory-like structure was to be the venue for the crowning of my art. 'Whatever became of good old-fashioned architectural embellishments like flower-pots, fountains and sculptures?' I thought, making my way inside.

The lobby was already teeming with delegates. In one corner stood the excited gaggle of African ladies I had seen at the High Commission reception. They waved gaily on seeing me; my fainting episode must have left a lasting impression. But why be so cheerful on so solemn an occasion? How the mighty had fallen! Innumerable were the times I had rehearsed this entrance, suitably late, triumphantly escorted by high-level diplomats, beaming benignly at the BBC cameras following my every move, and now here I was scuttling like an anonymous ant towards the registration desk.

One of the African ladies, a rather plump and homely figure with a broad nose and wide-lipped smile, joined me. Dressed in a pink batik caftan, she resembled African royalty.

She beamed when I told her so. 'Why, all your Indian ladies are like maharanis. That lovely silk they wear, is it called a sari?'

I promised to send her a few samples and asked to see the evening's programme. Despite grim hints, the African lady persisted in lingering on by my side and engaging me in social chit-chat. Thus those crucial minutes just before the start of the ceremony, which could have been used in making vital publishing contacts, were lost in listening earnestly to the monsoon situation in Tonga (which she politely informed me was not in Africa) and how similar in upbringing were the Tonganese to the Indians.

'We see all your films back home. The Quaker fathers have a video showing every month. Nargis, Raj Kumar . . . Why, he is such a gentleman.' She expertly rattled off the names in a kind of pidgin English, and seemed proud of being a recent graduate of the Open University.

'This is my first shot at writing. You know what those Quakers said, the good Lord bless them?' She prodded my ribs confidentially. '"Mrs Watanabe, you have a gift. It is your duty to share it."'

Strangely, Amma felt the same about my poetry.

'And to top it all, guess what?' Helpless, I looked at her. 'Quantas is flying me free. I am their Aborigine mascot for this year.' A wide, happy smile followed this nugget of information.

I needed to get away. 'But how fortunate for you. I do hope you gain at least some recognition in your homeland. And you must come and stay with us if you ever visit India,' I replied preparing to make my way to the toilets. 'Please excuse me, I must relieve myself. You know, the suspense.'

'Oh, you poor man, you are not in good health, are you? First fainting, now dysentery. Anyway, good luck to you and, as they say in Tonga, "Better being a healthy dog on four legs than a sick man on two."'

I thanked her for sharing this national wisdom and rapidly made my way towards the camera crew who had suddenly materialised. Who knew? Amma might well catch a glimpse of me on the *Doordarshan News*.

The crush of people in the lobby was getting unbearable. Dotted around at strategic intervals, I noted, were a few pale English faces, planted, no doubt, to give an air of authenticity to the event. This was, after all, London, the seat of the literary Empire. Several Chinese-looking individuals, wearing identical navy blue Mao suits, stood in one corner, in glum impenetrable silence. A general stampede was brewing around a table in the middle, where a sickly-looking brown liquid was on display in white plastic cups and a pile of tired samosas and spring rolls sat sulking in a corner.

There was no sign of Seth. It would no doubt be his usual last-minute VIP entrance, the signature shawl flapping round him like a triumphal banner, perfect smile trained on the television cameras. Having at last got hold of a drink, I retreated to a corner behind a pillar, slightly overwhelmed by the presence of so many international dignitaries.

Mrs Watanabe soon hunted me down. 'You know, there is something open and good about your face. Why, you could almost be one of us.'

I accepted the compliment grudgingly, and, succumbing to her insistent request, rapidly recited a verse from my poem 'Reflections on a Mother's Love'.

Mrs Watanabe clapped her hands in appreciation. 'I should have known! Your poem, like your face, is a wide-open window. Tell me, where are you sitting?' She seemed genuinely disappointed by the cruelty of the seating plan.

It was then that I espied Naina, minus Mr Mistry but with her new friend, the Irish priest. This friend was no doddering pious octogenerian limping painfully along. Striding by her side, with all the confidence of a lion cub, was a handsome man of not more than forty. The black robe he wore complemented the ruddiness of his cheeks, and his hair, which he wore slightly long, was the same colour as Naina's, brown with a hint of red. That Naina was enamoured of his teachings there was no question. It was obvious in the way she leaned affectionately towards him, smiling encouragingly every time he opened his mouth. They were swiftly ushered to the VIP seats by one of the pale faces.

I patiently dozed through the shadow-dancing puppets and the video on the bee-keeping traditions of Mali. From where I sat, right in the middle of the row and wedged between the Kenyan and the Bhutanese delegates, I could glimpse Naina's profile, engaged in animated conversation with the priest. As the clock ticked merrily to its destination and the hour of the announcement approached, the tension of the past days slowly uncurled within me like the release of that familiar tightly-clenched fist.

A sudden hush fell over the hall as the duke of some minor principality like Northumbria, a Patron of the Commonwealth Society, got up from the front row and climbed onto the podium. A distinguished Army type, the sort who sipped gin and tonic at the gymkhana, he gave a long and rambling speech about the brotherliness of the world, which was fast shrinking to the size of a village, all thanks to the wonders of the English language. So sincere and earnest did he sound that I almost held out my hand as a sign of fraternity to the stony-faced Bhutanese sitting to the right of me. I looked around the hall and failed to see Seth. What could be keeping him?

'And now I call upon the Right Honourable Mrs Mistry to announce the name of the fortunate winner of the thirty-fifth Commonwealth Prize for Poetry.'

And there in front of us stood Naina, smiling down imperiously at all the adoring upturned faces, opening a closed envelope with the knife-edge poise that characterised her every move.

'The proud recipient of this year's prize, I am pleased to announce' — my heart did a somersault and ended curled up somewhere near my left toe — 'is Mrs Watanabe from the Republic of Tonga.'

CHAPTER SEVENTEEN

A post-mortem with new friends

◡

THEY SAID THEY saw me wandering in a daze, thrusting my poems at everybody as they left the hall. I have no recollection of my antics that evening. I only hope I did not disgrace Amma's name by giving way to ridiculous displays of emotion in public. Not being that kind of man, I find it hard to believe that I was discovered sobbing Kamala's name in the Gents by none other than the Irish priest, who promptly deposited me at Naina's feet. Thus, once again the cruel twist of destiny found me at the Mistrys' residence, on the receiving end of sympathy and refreshments. Three cups of tea and four buttery biscuits later, things began to take a clearer shape.

'Is he any better? Poor chap, such a mortal blow'. The polished tones of Seth drenched me like a bucket of cold water. As always, he had taken a front-row position at my public stoning.

'Seth, I know how much you enjoy salting an open wound, but don't forget even you have turned out to be a loser today. In my case, the world has been denied the appreciation of an original, unheard voice. But tell me, with what face will you, the celebrity, now return to

India?' My venomous words came rushing out before I had a chance to edit them.

'Tut, tut, the vicious face of Mr Naidu. What a tragedy that such a "gifted" voice must remain unappreciated.' Seth looked at me with infinite pity. 'You simpleton. How long will it take you to understand that accolades of this kind function only as a minor irritant to someone of my standing? After all, how many trophies can one collect in a lifetime?' And, sighing, he lit one of his noxious French cigarettes.

Turning to Mr Mistry, he continued, 'With due respect, why do you think I chose to sit out the ceremony here in the company of Your Excellency? I knew all along it would be a half-baked dimwit from some far-flung heathen corner of the earth who would end up snaffling the prize. Why, I believe that Watanabe woman was barely able to string two words of English together in her acceptance speech?' Stretching his long limbs arrogantly, he got up and walked towards Naina, seeking an ally for his fascist views.

Seth's pontificating was unbearable. I turned to Mr Mistry for support. There he sat, the usual philosophical smile playing upon his lips, fingering his beard like a prayer bead. O'Brian by his side completed the cosy family picture.

'So much depended on this, sir. So many maternal hopes, a lifetime of struggle, wiped out in a single cruel moment.'

A teardrop fell silently into my tea. Mr Mistry patted my hand sympathetically and ordered me a fresh cup. I did not dare look at Naina. Her disappointment would have been too much to bear. How passionately had she believed in my talent, and here I lay, a confirmed failure, at her feet.

Her behaviour that evening puzzled me no end. Normally impeccably groomed, she sat looking tired and irritable, the folds of her sari like an untidy cloud around her. One hand impatiently fingered the necklace that encircled her throat like a string of stars, while every so often the other reached out and grabbed a cigarette from Seth. This image was not to my aesthetic liking. I definitely didn't approve of Indian women smoking. Quietly, I sneaked a glance at Mistry. What would he as a representative of Indian culture abroad make of this *fast* behaviour? But he continued to sit, calm and collected, while the two infidels steadily polluted the air around us with their nicotine smoke.

'Just listen to this, Seth. I mean, I am all for female emancipation but this seems just a little too pathetic.' Naina's husky voice read out Mrs Watanabe's winning entry:

> ' "It is the night-time moon
> that is my enemy . . . breeding flower and worm
> within my soul.
> Daytime sees the same old return to . . .
> feeding pigs and grinding corn . . ." '

Seth and Naina collapsed into fits of laughter as she shut Mrs Watanabe's book with a decisive hand.

'Is this the crowning glory of literature these days?' Seth looked at Mr Mistry with a scornful smile. 'And this woman claims to be the rightful heir to Shakespeare and T. S. Eliot. Why, even our Naidu here could pen a better line.'

With a loud snort, he strode towards the window, his shiny shoes gliding through the thick carpet like two eager alligators scenting their prey. Aware of the impressive picture he cut, he flung open the window, letting in the autumn night chill, and leaned upon the ledge, brows knitted in thought, skilfully flicking the ash from his cigarette onto the rosebush below.

Suddenly a soft musical voice rose in my defence. 'Actually, I quite understand the gentleman's plight, Mrs Mistry. The destruction of hope, as Christ himself tirelessly repeated, is one of the deepest causes of human suffering.' Of all people, it was O'Brian, the Irish priest, pleading my cause.

I warmed to him instantly. Up to now he had been but an anonymous, large blur of whiteness to me, but for the first time I took a good look at him.

I had not realised what a big man he was. His legs, crossed modestly at the ankle under the plain black gown he wore, obscured most of the intricate Persian embroidery of the sofa cover. Sitting next to him, Mistry looked like an underfed sparrow, in spite of being well above average Indian height. I looked at O'Brian gratefully. When all was said and done, he was a representative of God, after all. But what irritated me was the adoring way in which Naina beamed at his every word, with all the fervour of a recent convert. His pronouncement on the suffering of Christ was rewarded by her leaning forward and giving his hand a most friendly squeeze. Surely she could not be contemplating a conversion to Catholicism? What a predicament that would put her husband in.

Naina's actions were not lost upon Seth, who, hoping for some cheap camaraderie, kept giving me roguish winks, which I chose to ignore. My immediate worry was Mr Mistry's reaction to his wife's religious enthusiasms on the sofa. But he seemed intent on leafing through Mrs Watanabe's book, which lay like a burning match upon the sofa.

'Actually, Seth, there is surprising melody in some of her verse.' Mr Mistry's voice had acquired an energetic bounce not lost on me. 'I particularly like the sound of this. Listen.' And he read aloud:

> '"Your muscle-bound body
> Sleeping next to mine.
> How many stars have I
> woven on to your skin,
> Lying awake each night?"

'Shades of Shelley, don't you think, Seth?'

'Shelley? More like toilet shit, if you ask me.' Seth crudely dismissed Mr Mistry's generous compliment. 'I think Shelley would more likely approve of this.' He cleared his throat self-importantly and declaimed, each word a confident drumbeat echoing around the room:

> 'There was a carving of flesh
> At the marketplace that night.
> A division of spoils.
> The merchants were gathered to
> Plunder the gems. To toss up
> Between your heart and mine.
> Close by stood, the distance of a caress,
> Just beyond the rim of light,
> A pack of tall ships foaming at the mouth,
> Straining against the anchor tying them down.'

'Superb delivery', was all I could manage, while all around me the room burst into appreciative praise.

'Your "How the East Was Won" has always moved me, Seth,' Mistry said admiringly, and even O'Brian, who as the only colonial representative in the room ought to have looked guilty, came out with 'Stirring stuff'.

Seth merely nodded in acknowledgement and reached for another cigarette. 'What about you, Naidu?' He was back to the baiting game again. 'Were the sentiments too high-flown for you?'

'Not at all. I think you have managed to capture the essence of Imperialism most magnificently.'

My heroic reply, brimming over as it was with poetic insight and goodwill, astounded everybody. The winner takes it all, I thought, remembering the American song Feroze used to play repeatedly just before his exams. Not once had anyone in that room shown the same determined keenness on reading or discussing my work. And now, with the shadow of failure hanging over my head, what chance did my verse have of ever crossing a single village pond, let alone the seven seas?

> 'Failure, like a cloud of bees
> chasing me from the shade of the mango tree.
> Never again will I enjoy its fruit,
> for failure hangs above my head like a cloud
> of bees.'

I quietly murmured the lines to myself but the Irish priest, gifted as he was not just with soothing wisdom but with attentive ears as well, picked this up and asked me in a most kind voice, 'Tell me, Mr Naidu, was this poem a part of your submission for the competition?'

I nodded silently as treacherous emotions threatened again to flood my eyes. The lines I had been rehearsing for my acceptance speech came back.

'You see, Father,' I said, addressing him for the first time, 'I am but a helpless instrument in the hands of my pen.'

'My, my!' exclaimed Seth, alert to my every pronouncement. 'I believe our dear Naidu here has already penned his own epitaph. How useful to have a priest handy.' Naina giggled at this infantile display of wit and dragged deeply on her third cigarette.

I decided then and there to leave before my dignity took any further bruising. What would Amma's reaction be to all this ridicule being showered on her son?

'Please, sir, if you do not mind, I must be getting back to the hotel. I need to call home. My family will be waiting anxiously for the results.'

I hated dragging the family name into the middle of such a distinguished gathering, but I knew Kamala had been praying on my behalf to her favourite gods for the last fortnight and would break her fast only after my call.

Mr Mistry looked at me kindly, as a father would at a son. 'Of course, Naidu, we understand. But do stay for a while, there is no hurry. This notion of Seth's interests me . . . the politicisation of art. As you are an up-and-coming Third World poet, I would be interested in hearing your views on this ongoing colonial exploitation.'

'Sir' – I was desperate to leave – 'in my humble opinion it is not so much exploitation as luck that shapes our art. But please, I need to return to the hotel.'

Mr Mistry looked vaguely dissatisfied by my reply. No doubt he had been hoping for a fully-fledged, bare-chested round-table talk, but nobody seemed in the mood to indulge him.

'I have a suggestion,' he said. 'Why not call your family from here? The time there would be' – he peered at his watch – 'why almost five in the morning. Sure you don't want to wait a bit longer? They might be asleep.'

'No, sir, they will most definitely be awake. You see, Kamala, being a devoted wife, will be anxiously waiting for my news. There is a religious fast that she has observed.' I looked at him apologetically.

'Fast? Why, does she have a weight problem?' Naina, emerging from her private reverie, was quick to pick up on that. 'Really, these Indian women! When will they break free from the Stone Age? Fasting indeed. And for what? So you can go back and string some twopenny silver-plated medal like a noose round her neck?'

Mr Mistry lifted his hand to silence her while she smoothed the pleats of her sari with exaggerated movements, a frown of irritation creasing that lovely forehead.

Could it perhaps be the serpent of jealousy? Had the mention of Kamala's name kick-started it awake? Despite Naina's protestations to the contrary, her unnatural interest in me as a man could only go by the name of love. Her next words therefore came as a rude surprise.

'Come on, O'Brian, let's retire to the study. There are some religious lithographs I picked up in Perugia last year that I want you to see. You could help me with the

Latin text.' And with barely a nod to Seth and not so much as a backward glance or farewell to me, she strode out of the room, O'Brian following like an obedient pilgrim.

'Well, well, well.' Seth made an elaborate show of consulting his watch. 'Another one bites the dust, as the Americans say.' This in an enigmatic stage whisper. 'I think I, too, will be taking my leave. All this excitement in one day is not good for the old libido.' He winked at me theatrically. 'Like Naidu, I need privacy to lick my wounds. Besides, I have to be at my publisher's at the crack of dawn.'

'Have you brought out another book, Seth?' I asked suspiciously, determined to call his bluff. 'I thought you were meant to be on a "cerebral sabbatical" this year?'

I had lifted the phrase used by him in the *Indian Express*. Now, with Naina safely out of earshot, I felt more confident about tackling Seth and his delusions of grandeur.

'Well, since you are being so ultra-inquisitive, as a matter of fact it is Ostrich who asked me – I'm sure even you have heard of them, the UK's premier publishing group? They're keen on bringing out an anthology of this competition, a sort of cocktail of all the entries.' He looked straight at me. 'Naturally, given my experience and reputation, they're keen I should be involved right from the start as the editor. The final selection, you will be pleased to know, will depend entirely on me.' And without waiting for a reply, he made a swift exit from the room.

I waited till I heard the front door slam before bursting out, 'Just, just look at those double standards, sir.' Anger made my voice shake and I forgot all propriety. 'There he was, tearing poor Mrs Watanabe and the competition to bits, and now he is busy being its biggest promoter. Absolutely no scruples, sir. And absolutely no mention of including my submissions.'

'Well, Seth is a resourceful fellow,' Mr Mistry agreed. 'We have known him for years. In fact, it was he who introduced us to the arts. I always respect his judgement.' He wandered over to the side cabinet to pour himself another whisky.

Bent over the Johnny Walker bottle, Mr Mistry suddenly looked old and tired, beard drooping like a flag at half-mast, the bags under his eyes like pale, puffed-up pincushions, the type Kamala used when sewing Lord Ganesha's outfits. Ignoring my own misery for a moment, I almost reached out to hug him, so frail did he seem.

'Look here, Naidu, I don't like the idea of you slinking back to a lonely bed in that hotel. It has been a traumatic day for you. Why not spend the night here? You will be well looked after. Just make yourself at home in the blue room.'

*

The dreaded blue room. I could have found my way blindfolded, for was it not there that my senses had first been deflowered after languishing asleep for so many years? I briefly wondered about Naina: whether she would have the impudence to attack me again, or whether she was still engrossed in her inspection of the religious lithographs. Mr Mistry was right; she was a woman for all seasons, one moment stalking me like a berserk tigress, the next moment singing holy hymns.

The heavy mahogany door with the simple blue inlaid motif did not yield at first to my gentle push. Tired and increasingly dispirited, I gave it a firmer shove. But the door refused to open. Faint voices floated to me from a distance, and Naina's low-throated laughter bounced back from one of the dark, brooding walls. I decided to pass the night on the sofa in the drawing room.

It was a most uncomfortable sleep. The sofas, though extremely decorative and visually appealing, were not designed to lull a dispirited poet's limbs to sleep. I took the liberty of taking off my trousers and helped myself to one of Naina's shawls, which lay like a splash of red upon one of the armchairs.

My breathing kept time with the chiming of the clock that ticked away somewhere deep within the womb of the house. Strange muffled noises rose from time to time. At one point I heard the slow pit-pat of bare feet, the tinkle of glass and the swoosh of a wine-cork opening. These impressions were punctuated by visions of Kamala's wide, homely face staring at an empty plate. Once, like a character from *A Midsummer Night's Dream*, I even felt the warmth of a cheek pressed upon my eyelid. It was a most troubled sleep, coloured with the low, suppressed lilt of laughter and the memory of Mr Mistry's tired, drawn face.

I greeted the next morning with a stiff back and a nail-chewing headache. Squatting on his haunches and observing me with frank, untamed curiosity was the sparrow-like servant Ramu, wearing a crumpled pyjama whose loose drawstring lay like a sleeping snake upon the carpet. One of his hands caressed the Hoover crouching by his side in a state of suspended animation, while the other absent-mindedly picked his nose.

'*Chai*, Sahib? Bringing you some piping hot toast and bed-tea?'

'Nothing, nothing. I need to get back to my hotel most immediately.'

What if Mr Mistry was to find me lounging in his drawing room in this state of undress?

But before I could make good my escape, Naina entered the room, followed by another domestic bearing a tray. I was not the only one to have passed a restless night. Light circles of the palest violet bruised Naina's eyes. Her mouth seemed curiously swollen, and unruly strands of hair escaped from her hastily tied bun.

'Naina, please don't take my defeat so much to heart. You know, it is not such a blow after all. I did some hard thinking last night and do you know something, real talent will out. My mother always drilled that into my head when I was growing up, and that's how it will be. My poems, like the proverbial phoenix, will rise from the ashes.'

I looked at her brightly, hoping these words would pep up her spirits.

'What the devil are you wittering on about?'

With that she reached for her shawl and held it up to her nose. 'It stinks of you now. Ramu, send this for dry-cleaning, will you?

'By the way, Naidu' – she carelessly tweaked my cheek – 'we have decided to take you with us to Manchester. It will do you good to see the British hinterland.'

Why on earth was she using the royal 'we'? I wondered. Any pretext to keep me with her longer and abuse me further.

'I hate to disappoint you, Naina, but my visa runs out in three days' time and I refuse to be detained here as an undesirable alien.' I remembered the wording from the visa application form.

'Don't worry your literary head about such bureaucratic details, Naidu.' Mr Mistry stood before me, looking impeccable in a blue blazer and maroon stripy tie. I, in contrast, felt hopelessly underdressed and unwashed.

'O'Brian is quite right, Naina. I think a brief foray up north would be quite educational for our friend here. It's not every day that one has the chance to see industrialisation in action, and what better guide than Father O'Brian, who is an old Manchester hand?'

Manchester! The cradle of the Industrial Revolution. My poetry could only benefit by coming into contact with such a vibrant working-class city. 'Seize every opportunity in England, Kavi, explore the length and breadth of that beautiful island. Understanding the English psyche will be so beneficial to your poetry.' Amma's words bounced back into my mind.

'I am sure the visit will be most beneficial, sir. Thank you for allowing me to accompany you on your high-level trip.'

'Oh, but it is not I who will be going. Naina here and O'Brian have decided upon this. O'Brian seems to think your cultural tour of Britain will not be complete without a look at his centre. I am sure you will be well

140

looked after,' Mistry concluded and, shooting me another of those kind yet puzzled smiles of his, he disappeared from the room.

CHAPTER EIGHTEEN

A neglected man

~

MRS PEREIRA'S CONCERNED eyebrows met me at the door.

'But where in this revolving round earth have you been? We have been so worried, and your mother calling and pestering at least three times. Has she any idea of Greenvitch mean time? Can you imagine, disturbing holy sleep like that? I mean, we are hard-working Indians abroad. Not like the lazy bumsters back home. How am I supposed to know your where-abouts? I am not my lodgers' guardian angel, I say to her.' Her eyebrows were quivering with indignation by the time she finished.

No, I assured her, I had failed to win the prize, so had certainly not been carousing the night away with champagne and rosy-cheeked English girls. Yes, I still had every intention of writing poetry and would not retrain as a doctor or an accountant. Now, if she did not mind, could I please book a call to India and lay my poor mother's heart to rest?

Amma had called thrice. That meant three times at night would she have walked the potholed half mile to Balwant Rai's STD booth, through the insect-crowded pitch darkness of the washerwomen's *bustee,* and cajoled or bullied him into making the call. At her age, to walk alone in the thick of the night with all manner of undesirable elements lurking all around while I lingered in England, cocooned in the lap of cosy, self-indulgent sorrow. And Kamala? The ambulance would have reached the Holy Family Hospital by now. Kamala, suspended from a drip, would be gasping for droplets of glucose, devoted eyes beseeching the gods to reward a betraying husband. The tragedy of the human condition! Then and there I decided to address the issue in my next poem.

Seeing my agitation, Mrs Pereira surprisingly agreed to let me use her personal telephone. It was strictly against hotel rules, she informed me, leading the way to her office, and moreover she was extremely busy, what with the new academic term and all. Our journey to her office was, in fact, interrupted several times by harassed-looking students from the London School of Economics demanding an immediate reappraisal of their lodging terms and conditions.

'It is the start of the year, you see,' Mrs Pereira explained patiently. 'And each time it is the same sob story. How poor the situation is back home. The grandmothers waiting for life-saving bypasses and hernia removals in Houston. But' – and most triumphantly did she smile – 'proudly I can say I don't budge a penny.'

'Surely some Christian mercy wouldn't go unrewarded, Mrs Pereira?' I thought back to the Anglo-Indian ladies of the British Council who jangled an empty Quality Street box every Christmas for a retirement home in Dorset.

'Christianity be damned' was Mrs Pereira's blasphemous reply. 'Respect for money, that is what these fashionable colleges don't teach. No good cramming your head with numbers when you can't even count your own pennies. Tell me, should I lower my room rate so that they can go and blow it all away on some giggly blonde with more boobs than brain?'

Who would have thought that ticking away beneath that mother-of-pearl cross lay the heart of a social crusader?

Mrs Pereira's office, unlike the rest of the hotel, was a shrine to untidiness. Bills, receipts, magazine cuttings, old issues of the *Reader's Digest*, all fought for space on the large glass-topped desk, behind which hung a large portrait of what could only be the late Mr Pereira. Seen through the cloud of fingerprints that softly blurred his features, I could make out a friendly-looking individual with fleshy lips and the same amazing eyebrows. This maldistribution of facial hair was definitely a family trait, I thought, sneaking a quiet look at Mrs Pereira.

She must have lip-read my mind for she immediately responded, 'My dear late husband, that is who it is. We were second cousins, you know. I met him for the first time at a nephew's confirmation. I was sixteen, he twenty. He said he liked the yellow lace on my dress.' Most dreamily did those eyes then close as Mrs Pereira lifted her trademark cross and pressed it softly to her lips.

'Being related and all, the local priest refused to bless the union, and Mr Pereira, being the perfect gentleman, refused to fight the Church, so we did what any self-respecting second cousins in love do: caught the next boat to Southampton, with only five hundred rupees and an ocean of love to feed us. He died a year later. The cold here, it settled in his bones, just wouldn't budge.'

I reached out to touch her hand in sympathy. For an instant, I thought of Kamala and Feroze in a similar predicament. What if I was to catch pneumonia in London? They didn't even have a decent portrait of me to grieve over.

I must have held Mrs Pereira's hand for longer than necessary, for with a sudden jerk she pulled herself free.

'Okay, okay! We all survive, don't we? That damn painting always makes me feel senti.' She pulled out a lacy hanky from her housecoat and wiped the ends of her eyebrows delicately. 'Now, let us call your mother, before she has us cartwheeling again.'

'Sorry, all lines to Delhi are busy,' the nasal voice of the telephone operator kept repeating and I grimly imagined the news of my failure being wired into every available Indian ear.

At last Amma's voice came through, heavy with sleep. 'Is that you, Naidu? Don't worry, *beta*, we have heard the news. Mrs Basu went around the road telling everybody. We'll try again next year. The right connections weren't made this time.'

An enormous weight lifted from my heart. So the tragedy had not maimed her spirit. Amma's faith in my poetry still rang loud and clear.

'And Kamala? How is she? Have you been to the hospital, Amma?'

'Hospital? Why on earth should she be there? In fact she is getting plumper by the minute, it is all that ghee-soaked *prasad* she insists on frying.' Amma sounded irritated.

'Thank God, she has broken the fast at last. I am so relieved.' Pleased, I shouted back into the phone, which was becoming crackly again. At least my conscience was to be spared the failing health of a devoted wife.

'Fast? What fast? Oh, you mean for your success? Well, she couldn't keep it after all, could she? The dates weren't convenient. Some Hare Krishna Centre has just opened and she needs to be fit as a fiddle for all the functions. Anyway, when are you coming back? Miss Sinha from the Ministry keeps ringing up, says that Gupta is threatening the sack. No point in you hanging around now.'

Before I could reply to this barrage of questions, Mrs Pereira's hand came down on the receiver.

'Remember you are calling from London, not Gaziabad. At this rate no bill will be paid. You will plead poetic ignorance and catch the next flight home and I will be left holding baby, bathwater, tub and soap.'

How little faith Mrs Pereira had in humanity. But I suppose it was understandable. Losing Mr Pereira like that could turn anybody's heart to stone.

*

Back in my room, I thought over my telephone conversation. Kamala's betrayal bothered me the most. One little fast and she could not keep it, despite knowing how important it was for me to win the prize. She, who in the past would have eagerly skipped a meal a day for a month had I so much as cleared my throat. The temple *laddus* came first now. So much for wifely loyalty and support. I put away the timetable for return flights to Delhi. There was no need to hurry back. Rouse

146

Avenue merrily continued its daily tick-tock without me. As for the office, let Mr Gupta rave and rant; that job had never appealed to me, anyway. Only one thing remained. Quickly I took out my exercise book and scribbled a few lines.

> *I can bear the hurt of a thousand stones*
> *The betrayal of a thousand eyes.*
> *A thousand faces can fold away their smiles.*
> *I will not mind.*
> *But when a wife, a mother, a son, all unkind*
> *Do the same . . .*
> *Then all the perfumes of Arabia*
> *Will not soothe the hurt within my sighs.*

The poem, written from the heart, just flew from my pen. All I had to do was ensure it was posted to Delhi as speedily as possible. On impulse, I decided to make a Xerox copy for my own records. Kamala could never be trusted with paper.

On reaching reception, I found the sulky students from the London School of Economics still camped there, a few even smoking openly. No way was Feroze going for an overseas education, however much Amma might have set her heart on Cambridge. Look at the specimens this English education seemed to breed. One in particular was especially distasteful: a thin, dark fellow, who looked like a shady Bombay underworld character with overdressed hair and sideburns reaching down to the chin. A belt with a large brass buckle sat low round his hips, and the buttons of his overprinted shirt were open, despite the presence of elders, to reveal a smooth, girlish, slim neck. And the poor parents back home thought they were sending them to England to imbibe knowledge!

This flashy student sat perched on the check-in counter, deep in talk with Mrs Pereira in the most intimate fashion, as though she were a long-lost sister. She must have seen the disapproval on my face for she immediately burst into an explanation.

'Guess what? A Syrian-Christian like me. Why, he is from the same Madgaon district as me. Matthew Joseph, meet Mr Naidu, our most famous resident poet.'

'Please, Mrs Pereira, don't.' I wished she had not revealed my identity. I was in no mood to distribute autographs.

The boy stuck out his hand in a most familiar fashion. 'Naidu?' He scratched his left cheek thoughtfully. 'There was one Seth we did in class ten . . . but Naidu?'

'Please, Mrs Pereira, I am in a hurry. Could you please post this for me? It must reach Delhi urgently.' I held out the envelope with the poem to her, ignoring the boy, who was openly staring at me, still scratching away at that cheek.

'And stamps? I suppose like money they grow on trees. Overseas charges are now double under this government. Do you want this sent first class, second, by sea, air or land?'

How humiliating to negotiate postal charges in front of that rude boy.

'The quickest way possible, Mrs Pereira. Never mind the cost; please add it to my bill. Also, I will be away for a few days.'

I would normally have given a detailed outline of my whereabouts, requested tourist maps of Manchester, and listened in appreciative silence to Mrs Pereira's authoritative insights into that city. But today was different. Mrs Pereira irritated me for some reason; maybe it was the boy who was refusing to budge his bottom from the counter.

'Catching up on your sightseeing, then. High time too. Are you taking a coach trip to Scotland? My advice would be to focus on the lakes. Indians from back home love it always, they say it is so like a mini-Kashmir. But I say to them, you can keep your lakes and mountains, just give me back the coconut water from my Madgaon any day.' Mrs Pereira's knowledgeable voice followed me as I headed for my room again.

*

Having packed my belongings, I waited downstairs for Father O'Brian to pick me up. Still feeling a little wounded and sensitive, I was glad that the lobby was now deserted, with no sign of the ever-vigilant Mrs Pereira.

Suddenly, Matthew Joseph reappeared, shamelessly naked but for a blue striped towel round his waist. A toothbrush dangled from his lips. Ignoring me, he went behind the desk and helped himself to some stationery.

'So you have moved in here. I thought the rates were too high for you students?' I rarely stooped to sarcasm, preferring the honest, direct approach, but there was something about this boy which brought out my ugly side.

'Oh, it's you. Didn't even notice you. Sorry, were you saying something about hard up students?' And he smirked, his mouth a froth of mint-white.

I nodded grimly.

'You must know about hardship, being a poet and all that. As for me, remember the Madgaon connection, so don't feel sorry for me,' he said with another laugh.

Before I could work out the insolence behind this cryptic remark, the well-meaning figure of Father O'Brian appeared in the doorway.

Suddenly life was moving forward at breakneck speed. Delhi one day, London the next, and now Manchester beckoned. Mr Mistry was right. Maybe in Manchester I would find the right audience for my verse, forget the humiliation of the Commonwealth bid.

CHAPTER NINETEEN

The journey north

⌐❁

THE PRICKLY, SILVERY slant of rain, an old Guru Dutt melody playing on the radio and Naina's pale, ring-burdened fingers tapping on the car window. Father O'Brian drove swiftly and expertly, assuring us we would reach Manchester well before midnight.

I complimented him on his driving ability. 'The English are such jack of all trades. You can sing a hymn, drive a car, and even fry an egg, all in the same breath. Back home, no way would a pandit do anything but ring the temple bells. And even for that he would demand a donation. Don't you think so, Mrs Mistry?' I asked, hoping to draw Naina into the conversation.

Naina, in one of her self-absorbed silences, was humming along to a song on the radio. 'I think Patrick's list of accomplishments extends even beyond that. What do you say, eh?' And she reached over to ruffle O'Brian's hair playfully.

It was good that they had become such close friends in so short a time. Perhaps the company of a religious man would prevent her from making any more predatory advances to me.

'Please, Naina,' said O'Brian, 'there is a time and a place. Tell me some more about yourself, Mr Naidu.'

He turned to me with a smile so open and embracing that I was convinced he had been personally blessed by Our Lady. 'Tell me, what brings you to England? You strike me as a genuine man. Surely it must be more than the competition?'

His accent was so foreign, the words flowing musically fast, wrapped up tightly in each other, that I had difficulty in following his remarks, but Naina kindly repeated them at a more leisurely pace.

I considered his query carefully. 'It is very kind of you, Father, to think so highly of me.' Emotion made my voice quiver. The first genuine admirer I had met in England, and he had to be Irish. I looked out of the window, too moved to speak.

When I had recovered my poise, I went on, 'The idea of England has always fascinated us back home. For us this country represents all that is cheerful and dynamic in the human spirit. But' – my mind went back to the Weinbergs and the sadness swimming in Lady Weinberg's eyes – 'but I am not so sure now.'

Father O'Brian continued with his wise observations. 'You know, going back to this Commonwealth Prize, it always puzzles me that people are willing to accept an outsider's estimate on the value of their art, particularly those from the developing world. All I know is that it is one's inner self-esteem that ultimately matters, and the world can go hang itself.' Keen, concerned eyes, the colour of blue oceans in Government of India tourist brochures, assessed me in the rear-view mirror.

First-rate sentiments, no doubt, but the naïvety of the man was frightening. Must be the fault of religion. Didn't Marx say it was an opium that dulled the brain? Kamala had the same blinkered opinion: stay at home with bowed head and folded hands, and the publishers will form a courteous queue outside your door.

'Father, I am afraid this philosophy could prevail only in a monastery. In the real world, somewhere like India, it's who you know that counts. Take the example of Seth, the gentleman you met earlier in Mrs Mistry's house. That fellow is an absolute crook! In ten minutes flat, he becomes the best friend of every Minister he meets. And the net result? His poems are on the syllabus of every tenth-standard class from Ladakh to Lakshwadeep.'

Naina, who had been listening silently to this earnest exchange, burst out impatiently, 'I knew the talk would come back to Seth. Never miss an opportunity to attack him, do you, Naidu? And, after all, how is he different from you? The same set of oversexed, middleaged glands, that's all.'

We both laughed politely at her description, but privately I was shocked. Where was her sense of decorum in front of a priest?

The rest of the journey passed in amicable silence. I must have dozed off, for the next thing I knew, the countryside had been left behind and the bright lights and noises of a city surrounded us. The radio was humming soft instrumental music and, as my eyes sleepily readjusted to my surroundings, I half imagined a curious dance of hands unfolding in the front. Each time Father O'Brian changed gear, Naina's hand would descend upon his for the briefest of instants, and gently stroke it.

We soon reached Longsight. Father O'Brian had poetically described it as a deprived area of Manchester where 'lost souls huddle together for comfort and solace', but it looked prosperous enough to me. There were no beggars or cows loitering on the roads or nosing through the garbage, no sleeping families littered the clean pavements, and the houses built of brick seemed solid enough. The St Patrick Refuge for Battered Women was situated here. It was redbrick hostel-type accommodation similar to the YMCA back home. The English fondness for this cheerful red in their building material was truly touching, given the all-round greyness of their climate.

An elderly English lady wearing a checked apron and furry slippers let us in. She was introduced as Miss Haworth, the housekeeper. While O'Brian conferred with her, and Naina went to the Ladies, I inspected my surroundings. The hall smelled of cooking, and the walls were covered with welcome posters in several languages. I could make out the Gujerati, Hindi, Bengali and Urdu scripts among others. A large advertisement for a hairdressing diploma course was helpfully pinned near the telephone and I was reading the section concerning tuition fees when Naina reappeared, looking highly perturbed.

'No, no tea for me, thank you'. She waved aside the cup into which O'Brian was pouring steaming water from a kettle chained to the reception desk. A slow frown was beginning to wrinkle her forehead.

Father O'Brian, by contrast, seemed in his element, helping himself to a biscuit while flicking through the pages of *Reader's Digest*.

'Look, Naina, there's a wonderful cottage available for rent next summer in Iona off Scotland. Elementary comforts, but you wake up to the sound of the ocean each morning.' He pushed the open page towards her.

Naina waved her hand dismissively. 'What sort of a barbaric place have you brought me to, Patrick? You know I'm not accustomed to such shabby surroundings. I can't pretend to play Florence Nightingale in prehistoric conditions.'

I quite agreed with Naina's judgement. This place, with its one brown sagging sofa and stained carpet, was hardly fit for a VIP talk on sisterly solidarity. And this was meant to be the visitors' room, the show-piece of the centre. The English, so perfect in their prose, showed surprisingly careless hygiene at times. I thought back to the strenuous Dettol-scrubbing of the verandah that Kamala supervised every morning at home.

Unfortunately, O'Brian refused to take Naina's comments in the right spirit. A slow red climbed from his neck to his cheeks. Even his hands became pinker. It was my first non-textbook blush and I was amazed by his skin's ability to change colour to reflect the changing mood. We Indians possessed no such chameleon gift. Our eyes and mouth remained the only windows to the soul.

'I don't know quite what you had in mind, Naina, but as you wish. I would hate to ruffle your delicate diplomatic feathers.' O'Brian gave a sarcastic smile and refilled his cup. 'I think we had better arrange for you to be picked up. Perhaps you will feel more charitable in the morning.'

'Perhaps' was her noncommittal reply. The old alertness returned as she swiftly opened her small silk purse and extracted a thick official-type diary. 'Mrs Paisawala, the big fish in the little Indian pond here, should be picking me up any minute now. It would,' and here

Naina put on a thick Jullandari accent, 'be an honour were I to grace her humble abode.'

Barely had she finished speaking when, with an authoritative knock on the front door, Mrs Paisawala along with her husband and son appeared on the doorstep, ready to escort Naina to their house. Mrs Paisawala, large and fleshy-featured, wearing too many diamond rings on one hand and an ornate wedding-reception sari, made straight to where Naina was sitting and gave a deep Japanese-bow-cum-*namaskar*. Husband and son, both of the same stocky build, with identical hennaed haircuts and black over-tight leather jackets, remained standing by the door, the son throwing a musical key-chain into the air. It burst into a different Christmassy tune each time he caught it. Miss Haworth, O'Brian and I were ignored by the trio. How infinitely more refined was my family, with its gracious Indian upbringing.

Through the open door I could see a long yellow car – the latest Mercedes, O'Brian informed me – lying low on the road like a panther ready to pounce. Naina disappeared, throwing us extravagant flying kisses, shawl slipping from her shoulders so that her slim, creamy arms decorated with a single ivory bangle caught the light. I saw both the husband and son stare at her with sudden manly interest while Mrs Paisawala, her face one large U-shaped smile, was escorting Naina down the steps. I heaved a sigh of relief; at least tonight I would be spared her amorous advances.

It was a long, uncomfortable night in a modest, unremarkable room.

This trip to Manchester was turning out to be more about testing my cold threshold than about widening my literary experience. How could the women sheltering in this refuge even begin to understand my poetry? Once again, Naina was duping me with false promises of literary glory worthy of five-star surroundings. And here I lay staring disconsolately at the stern picture of Mother Mary on the wall. Father O'Brian, with whom I was sharing the room, kept up a steady snore which broke the stillness of the dark. If the boss had such frugal amenities, I shuddered to think about the others. I had as yet failed to see any of the battered women. They were meant to be in bed by nine, Miss Haworth had informed me, since the central heating was switched off then. There was no sign of any heating where I lay. The sheets were itchy and cold and a light draft kept brushing my cheek. I put on my socks, and after a moment of hesitation pulled on my trousers over my pyjamas. O'Brian slept on, stripped to the waist, the reddish hair on his chest rising and falling rhythmically.

Naina arrived the next morning, VIP late, good humour restored. She was at once surrounded by a group of excited women, showing her their embroidery, their home-made chutneys, their certificates in hairdressing. Father O'Brian and Miss Haworth looked on proudly, smiling happily, whispering the case histories of the women from time to time.

'That woman there, the one in the pink *salwar*-suit. Yes, she's Indian. Her husband tried to kill her last year, emptied a can of petrol over her head while she slept. And Maria over there . . .' Miss Haworth walked briskly over to a small, wheat-complexioned lady and abruptly whipped up her dress sleeve. The entire arm was fingerprinted with ugly, dark bruises. 'The boyfriend's an alcoholic. Pushed her and the child around when he'd had one too many.' Miss Haworth nodded wisely, saying all this in a matter-of-fact All-India Radio news bulletin sort of voice.

The women were eager to show Naina their hobby room, and I was left alone with O'Brian.

'So much suffering in this world,' I said. 'It makes me want to weep, and it is their near and dear ones committing these atrocities. You are a noble man, Father. Where would they be without you?' I thought of the hardships he endured and reached out to give him a warm, brotherly hug.

'We all have our crosses to bear. There are thorns everywhere, Naidu, that's why it's so important to grasp any loving hand that is extended, no matter which,' O'Brian replied, offering me a Mars Bar.

Naina reappeared moments later, cheeks flushed and radiant with success. 'Guess what? They think I'm a film actress from Bombay, keep asking for my autograph. Isn't that simply delicious? Wait till I tell Mistry. He'll find it so surreal.'

I was beginning to find her enthusiasms a little sad. Being compared to *Hema-Malini* obviously meant more than being a diplomatic high-flyer.

There they all were again, flocking round us like over-excited birds, representing every shade of grief. When I, rather ashamed of my earlier uncharitable sentiments, took up Father O'Brian's offer to recite to them some of my poems, there was a spontaneous burst of applause, so genuine it brought a tear to my eye. This was the stoicism of the human spirit, the ability to celebrate while holding back one's tears.

The poem 'Mother and Child' lay in my hand, but what came out was something entirely different, purely extempore.

> 'Your upturned faces
> Like fresh-cut flowers
> Trodden by a million feet.
> The wounds in your heart
> A necklace of thorns
> You silently weave.
> Arise, my sister. Arise.
> And stride once more towards the Sun.'

I would have continued but for the tears coursing down my cheeks. The sentiments expressed were too deep to be handled rationally. I looked at the ladies, who stared back understandingly. How brave and attentive they were. Not one sniffle or sob broke the pin-drop silence. Eventually, the wheat-complexioned lady, the one with the bruised arm, stepped forward and kindly offered me her handkerchief. Of Naina and O'Brian there was no sign. Overcome by feeling, they had discreetly slipped out of the room.

Miss Haworth, Anglo-Saxon to the bone, frowned at this display of untidy Indian emotion and quickly hustled the women out of the room.

'Really, Mr Naidu, as though they need reminding,' she said, turning off the lights, lips shut tight with disapproval. 'The girls were wanting something racy. You know, a catchy love song.'

*

That evening Mrs Paisawala threw a party in Naina's honour and reluctantly included us in the invitation.

Driving to her house in a south Manchester suburb was like passing through one of those exclusive Delhi neighbourhoods where well-bred Alsatians cautiously sniffed your clothes. There was a profusion of well-trimmed hedges and bushes, and even Naina exclaimed in delight on seeing some of the gardens glimpsed through large wrought-iron gates.

Mrs Paisawala's house resembled an Arabian-cum-Greek palace with a long driveway and fountains in the shape of peacocks and mermaids. I praised the beauty of the star-shaped flowerbeds and the alabaster statues of Greek mythological figures, but Naina curled up her nose, saying it all stank of new money.

'Do you know something, Naidu? Good taste can never be purchased. And guess what has paid for this?' The wide sweep of her arm included the garden, the house, the large shining antenna posing self-importantly on the roof. 'Size 34C bras and white lace panties, all one hundred per cent polyester!' She burst into a hoot of laughter.

'There is dignity in every type of labour,' O'Brian replied seriously, though I could spot his ears changing colour.

'Even selling nylon underclothing in bulk?' she asked, before collapsing once more in a peal of laughter.

Naina was immediately swallowed up by a group of loudly dressed ladies who pushed her towards a sort of dance floor in the middle of the drawing room, where shiny glass statues, European paintings and Chinese rugs fought for space. The latest Hindi disco music was playing and I saw a few middle-aged men, whisky glasses in hand, silk shirts unbuttoned, shaking their hips to the song. It was a cheerful gathering, with a lot of laughter. Plate upon plate of steaming non-vegetarian food was being circulated among the guests by young, frightened-looking English girls wearing short black skirts.

Having lost Naina, I searched for O'Brian and found him sitting comfortably between two elderly ladies wearing huge diamond studs in their noses and maroon *chappals*. Delicately holding a *pakora*, he seemed deep in conversation, but he soon spotted me.

'Come over, Naidu.' He gestured to me gaily. 'I am informing these ladies about our Centre. Do you know, they were not even aware of its existence till today, and we have been operating for some twenty years now.'

The ladies looked relieved to see me, and after a quick 'How are you, son? Have some more *paneer tikka*' to me in Punjabi, they vanished into the kitchen.

'You frightened them,' I teased O'Brian. 'Why spoil their evening by introducing social issues?'

The rest of the time passed in nodding, smiling and over-eating the starters. Mrs Paisawala, it seemed, was known for her lavish parties and a thick press of men hovered knowledgeably about the bar area, while women wearing their wedding best monopolised the seating.

'Have a drink,' the hospitable Mr Paisawala kept coming round and saying. 'It's champagne, Dom Perignon brand, the best of the French.' His hair, freshly hennaed for the occasion, glowed richly red under the chandelier, which would have outshone Billo's any day.

I tried to describe my vocation, ready to recite a verse or two, to the few men who attempted conversation, but the interest was temporary once it was established that I was not in import-export and lived in Delhi, not

London. I was edged out, and the talk went back to comparing notes on the best airline upgrade and five-star hotel deal in the Far East.

I gave up and went back to O'Brian. 'Brindians all,' I said, pleased with my use of Naina's term. 'Please don't judge all Indians by this party. When you come to Delhi, I will show you what a true cultured Indian is. We discuss politics and music and the future of our children in a changing world. All this is pure *tamasha*, as they say in Hindi. You follow? Just showbiz.'

O'Brian patted my shoulder and smiled. 'You're too harsh, Naidu. These "Brindians" also have their demons. Let them forget it in song and dance.' He paused reflectively. 'Remember, they are thousands of miles from home. There is homesickness in their blood and every day is a brand-new battle needing to be won. I am Irish, I know something about that.'

We left at midnight, the party still in full flow. The sweetmeats were yet to be served and the music kept getting louder and louder. But we had an early start back to London the next morning.

Naina, creature of contrasts that she was, insisted on accompanying us back to the Centre. She said she was tired of the electric blanket and automatic tea-making facilities in Mrs Paisawala's guest-room. I merely smiled and said nothing, though deep within me the alarm bells had started ringing. Was another amorous ambush being planned? But then again, perhaps the sight of the suffering women at the Centre had reformed her and she was contemplating a life of good works.

'An old Irish hymn?' Naina asked O'Brian, who was humming cheerfully as he drove.

I said, 'You really are a creature of God, Father. He never leaves your thoughts even for a minute, does He?' I hoped this religious reminder would encourage Naina's own moral turn-about.

'God is the farthest thing from my mind at the moment, Naidu,' she replied, reckless with drink. 'It is flesh I want, long arms snaking in and around me, somebody's mouth screaming undying love.'

'Phew!' said O'Brian. 'Spoken with passion like a true poet, Naina. Very evocative, I must say. By the way, Naidu, you must let me have a look at your poems one of these days.' His kindness was truly overwhelming.

I was to sleep in the hall, they explained patiently when we reached the Centre. It was not fitting that Mrs Mistry, given her status, should pass the night on a sofa in the entrance hall. A certain etiquette needed to be observed; besides, it was only a few hours before the drive back to London.

'Only to straighten the back,' Naina said, eyes moist with repentance, retiring into O'Brian's room.

I understood as only a poet could. But a strange restlessness refused to leave me. Poetic inspiration kept swimming to the surface, demanding to be heard. Naina's changed and penitent behaviour had sown the seeds for a new poem I intended calling 'The Fallen Have Risen'. I tiptoed to O'Brian's room intent on making them hear my latest creative outburst.

> Just as Mary Magdalen,
> Fallen to her knee,
> So you too shall bow
> For the World to see.

It is never too late
To stand at the Lord's Gate.

The door must have been locked, for it refused to open. Then I heard them, the sharp, urgent sounds leaking through the door, like an animal nursing a hurt. Concerned for Naina's well-being, (she had been drinking steadily through the evening), I banged loudly on the door.

O'Brian eventually opened it. 'Who the devil is there, disturbing the sleep of honest folk?' His voice was belligerent, with no trace of Irish softness.

He stood in front of me, milk-washed white, as naked as the day he was born, eyes still bleary with passion, mouth still bruised with love. And I at last understood.

CHAPTER TWENTY

A concerned well-wisher

～

WITH NAINA'S DISHONOURABLE conduct preying on my mind, I decided to cut short my stay in England and return home, back to my teakwood desk, my evening walks past the washerwomen's *bustee*, my daily verbal duels with Mr Gupta at the office. Despite the nobility of England's people and history, I was not cut out for the decadence of a country where married women seduced single-minded priests and intriguing liaisons were conducted behind cups of tea.

To escape from these disturbing emotions, I had of late cultivated the habit of frequenting the British Museum, which was but a stone's throw from the Ascension Modern Hotel. Preserved there were a few letters of Shelley's which made one's blood stir in excitement. Who knew but that one day my carefully crafted thoughts would find a place alongside them?

I felt I was walking in the exalted footsteps of scholars past and future as I handed in my blazer to the bright-eyed girl in the museum cloakroom. True to the Anglo-Saxon tradition, she always greeted me with meteorological observations regarding the prevailing conditions. A PhD student in music, she was supplementing her meagre allowance with this menial job. Back home a similarly qualified girl would sooner commit *sati* than dirty her hands in manual labour like this. But we were still stuck in Stone Age prejudice, while enlightened England moved ahead in leaps and bounds.

'*How is the poet of India doing? Be warmly in touch.*' Mrs Watanabe's curiously worded postcard lay waiting for me after one such visit. I decided to ignore the summons and requested Mrs Pereira to reconfirm my reservation with Air India. My English sojourn was proving a fiasco, with my poems still hibernating in the drawer, unrecognised, unacclaimed. I was in a foreign land with fast-depleting funds, away from the gentle ministrations of wife and mother. The future looked unpromising, dark and bleak.

There was something different about Mrs Pereira these days, a new softness I had noticed since my return from Manchester. The harsh orange housecoat she habitually wore had been replaced by a frilly peach-coloured frock. Her hair, previously tied in an unflattering ponytail, now framed her face in a girlish frizzy cloud, balancing those Brezhnevian eyebrows. Normally an astute observer of her guests, she failed to question me on the highlights of my Manchester trip and agreed, rather surprisingly, to let me ring home.

'You can please add that to my bill, Mrs Pereira.'

'No need for that, Mr Naidu. This call will be on the house. After all, you are almost a family member by now.'

Where was the mercenary negotiator of old? I looked at her closely. Something was most definitely black in the lentil soup.

'By the way, there is a small favour I am demanding.' Mrs Pereira's finger paused in front of a column in her accounts. 'You know your room, how peaceful and quiet it is, facing the back alley and all that? Well, Matthew Joseph – remember the boy from Madgaon? – he needs to do some serious studying with exams coming up. What do you say to swapping rooms?'

I looked at her in surprise. 'Really, Mrs Pereira. I thought you didn't want to encourage these vagabond student types. Whatever happened to your business principles?' Normally deferential, I was purposely impolite today.

'Well, he is a different cuttlefish, you know. From my own part of the world.' She paused and a smile slowly travelled from her lips and settled somewhere deep in her eyes. I knew then that Mrs Pereira was in love. Long, lonely years of grimly hugging the mother-of-pearl cross to her chest had given way to this irrational longing for a boy young enough to be her son.

Caught up as I was by this astounding revelation, I failed to notice the arrival of Mrs Watanabe. Suddenly she was there, dwarfing the lobby with her scarlet robes, a cheerful smile playing on her large, well-defined lips. So impressive was she that even Mrs Pereira was dazzled and rushed away to produce her special masala tea for the visitor.

'Ah, my long-lost friend!' cried Mrs Watanable. 'I manage to find you, then. So boring these poetry victories are, are they not? Suddenly you can't breathe alone and I say to myself, let me seek out my wise young friend from the East. He will give me solace in these troubled, celebrated times.'

Two *gulab-jamun* brown arms enfolded me and I could feel the soft, mattress-like bounce of her motherly bosom.

Noticing my downhearted expression, Mrs Watanabe suggested lunch.

'The only solution for underground spirits, my friend. As they say in Tonga, "Better a happy pauper on two legs than a wealthy king six feet underground."' Indian curry, she informed me as we waited for a taxi outside the hotel, was much appreciated in Tonga, especially the pork version with chips and runner beans.

Just as we were entering our taxi, we saw Seth come out of an expensive-looking shop. Accompanying him was a striking young girl with red hair, dressed in a miniskirt. Little did I know it then, but that girl would come to play an important role in my life.

'Cheap womaniser,' I muttered angrily as the taxi edged out. 'The fellow has no shame, romping around in broad daylight.'

'But what do they see in him?' Mrs Watanabe joined me in the attack. 'He does not upset my fancy at all. No squeezable flesh. In Tonga we often say, '"Better bed a papaya that breaks you than a cucumber that slides in like a bone."' One plump hand came down and poked my belly.

'Please, please. You are like my elder sister,' I remonstrated, as her touch grew more ticklish.

'Yes, yes, and can't I play with my little brother?'

Without a specific destination in mind, we left the choice of restaurant – it was my first Indian restaurant meal in England and expectations were high – to the Nigerian taxi driver, who dropped us in front of a small, heavily curtained establishment with a poster of the Taj Mahal in the window. The neighbourhood looked decidedly rough, with groups of non-English-looking children lounging in front of a newspaper shop, aimlessly kicking an empty Coke can. A few foreign women chatted away in a corner, pushing battered prams, while a man sat on the pavement, holding a bottle of beer.

The interior of the Raj Kamal Tandoori was night-dark. A tired-looking Bengali waiter, almost as dark as Mrs Watanabe, sulkily led us to a table near the window. We were the only customers. The *baigan bhartha* was out of season, but yes, pork curry with chips could be provided. Mrs Watanabe's face lit up, but my spirits sank.

Having consumed the *papad* and the toxic mint chutney, I decided to bare my soul. After all, Mrs Watanabe had led a fairly experienced life. Her feminine shrewdness would provide the right insight into Naina's despicable behaviour. As the curry was consumed and the *lassi* drunk, Mrs Watanabe pronounced her satisfaction and ordered some beer. Shocked, I reminded her that alcohol was strictly an after-sunset drink.

She laughed cheerfully at my concerns. 'My friend, even Jesus needed a glass of wine at breakfast, to polish his miracles.' And she forced me into sharing a glass.

The previous hour had passed in an extensive summary of her life in Tonga: the cornbread factory where she worked during the day, and where she had lost a toe at eighteen, the Open University tapes she listened to at night to blot out the sound of a snoring husband.

'Know something, Naidu?' A look of biblical revelation came over Mrs Watanabe's face. 'It was those tapes that did it. Opened the doors. Ah, these English poets.' She bowed her head reverently. 'Why, some of them can burst the buttons off one's dress.'

I nodded in agreement. My sentiments exactly, even if crudely put.

'Listen!' She snatched hold of my hand. 'I even wrote a poem on those Open University tapes.' Without waiting for my go-ahead, she launched headlong into it.

'The humming of the tape at night.
The noise competing with the stars so bright.
Shook awake dreams in a poor woman's breast.
Suddenly this barren life became a treasure chest.'

I smiled weakly, thinking of Seth's scathing words. That was the calibre of poetry that won prizes these days.

'He is a good-for-nothing is my man Macdonald, pants always on fire,' Mrs Watanabe concluded her life history sadly, wringing the last drop of heat from the warm once-white towels the waiter had reluctantly brought for us to wipe our hands.

'What's wrong with you, Naidu? You hardly ate.' The half-hearted way in which I was playing with the *pilau* had registered at last.

The beer was by now playing reckless games with my head. The moment was right for sentimental disclosures.

'Mrs Watanabe, I think I am at an emotional crossroads. You know, committed to one woman but being pursued by another most undesirable one.' How I

170

hoped she would be able to understand the high-flown emotions involved.

There was a sharp intake of breath and Mrs Watanabe looked fearfully at the waiter, who stood scowling by the door. 'But I am happily married, man!' she said. 'Got grown-up kids. Youngest daughter studying dentistry in Adelaide. Impossible for me to bed you, even though we are far away from near and dear eyes.'

'No, not you, Mrs Watanabe.' Really, the idiotic imagination of the woman! 'You are like an elder sister. It happens to be' – I lowered my voice discreetly – 'the wife of a top-ranking diplomat.'

'Does she love you, then?' I had caught her interest.

'Her actions say it, but not her words.' I thought of O'Brian. 'But these actions are also directed towards other unobtainable men.'

'You mean she sleeps with you as well as other men?'

I wished Mrs Watanabe would speak in a softer voice. The waiter was dusting an ashtray at the next table.

'Don't tell me.' Mrs Watanabe slapped the table excitedly. 'And I am Sherlock Holmes. Is it that Indian woman who handed me the prize, that snobby-looking one? Why, I saw her with Seth the other day, walking together skin to skin, tight together like twins.' She giggled at the image.

'Impossible!' I cut her short rudely. 'Seth can't stand her. In fact, he warned me about her.' It had been a mistake to confide in such a simpleton.

'So you are upset she is loving with other men. Why does it matter to you? As they say in Tonga, "Better an unfaithful wife with new tricks up her skirt than a loyal woman with two legs clamped shut."'

171

Shocked by her loose morality I shook my head emphatically, as did the waiter, who threw me a look of solidarity.

'No, no, no. That may be true of your country. But we Indians, we have our own code of ethics. It is an ancient civilisation, you know. We respect our marriage vows.'

Mrs Watanabe looked at me as she would at her dentistry-studying daughter. 'Tell me, Naidu, you are married, aren't you? I remember you telling me your educational worries about a son. So there is your wife on one side and your Indian moral code on the other. Now, was this code snoring under the bed when you and the snobby one were busy breaking the mattress?'

'This restaurant closes three-thirty p.m. sharp.'

Relieved, I looked up to see the waiter standing at our table, bill in hand, scowl on forehead. I did not like the turn the conversation had taken. How dare Mrs Watanabe imply that I had secretly enjoyed Mrs Mistry's unsolicited attentions?

With a satisfied burp, my lunch companion got up. 'We need to speak again, my confused friend. Your heart is pointing East to your wife, and your trouser bump is pointing West.'

She gave a rich laugh, the scarlet dress flapping after her as she squeezed into a waiting taxi.

CHAPTER TWENTY-ONE

A letter is sent

MRS WATANABE'S SARCASTIC words haunted me. It was time to stop being a hypocrite. Naina might have pursued me with unbridled passion, but, as Mrs Watanabe had potently observed, 'No woman can loosen a man's trousers single-handed.' Granted, Naina was momentarily distracted by poor Father O'Brian, who was confusing physical love with spiritual salvation. But this had to stop. First a poet, then a priest; who would be next?

I decided to write Naina a letter, something I should have done long before. A letter conveying at great length my disappointment that a woman of her stature should stoop to such carnal folly. The passing years have blurred the exact words I wrote that long-ago afternoon, but I remember the sinking sun lengthening its pinstriped shadows over my room, while Mrs Pereira's Hoover dutifully chewed the dust in the corridor outside.

Sparing no detail, I elaborated on how Naina had robbed me of my innocence in the blue room, and then, despite my protestations, continued with her sexual harassment, about which Seth, whatever his malevolent qualities, had given me a warning hint in a spirit of brotherly co-operation. I ended by describing the shameful episode in Manchester, where I had been taken as an unsuspecting decoy in order that Naina and Father O'Brian might give in to their mutual lust.

The denouement left me emotionally exhausted, and, having posted the letter in a discreet brown envelope, I waited anxiously for Naina's reaction. Her actions described so eloquently in black and white were sure to stab her conscience. Unwilling to leave the hotel lest she call with a heartfelt apology, I loitered within the dull confines of the lobby, enduring the sneers of the abominable Matthew Joseph, who had appointed himself Mrs Pereira's guardian angel and shadowed her every move.

Naina was silent for a week. Unable to bear the waiting any longer, I rang her the next day, trembling and tense with expectation. How would she react? With tears of remorse or with coarse indifference?

When she eventually came to the phone, she sounded reluctant and irritable. 'Naidu! I had quite forgotten about you. There have been so many distractions lately. Tell me, are you itching again for it?' The dangerous playfulness had returned to her voice.

'But haven't you read my letter?' I asked, my tension growing. 'I am ultimately a decent family man. I cannot allow you to play with my emotions any more. Mrs Watanabe has opened my eyes.'

Naina ignored this impassioned speech. 'Tell me, are you aching all over for me? And what bloody letter are you talking about? Don't tell me you've been penning poems to my beauty again?'

I put down the phone feeling nauseous. The letter, the crucial messenger of my intentions, had obviously not reached her. It had gone missing, swallowed up in some diplomatic black hole, being fingered by greasy, unscrupulous hands.

This was a nightmare. My letter in the wrong hands would be a walking-talking All-India Radio bulletin. Entire governments might fall, were a snooping journalist to find it. And Mr Mistry? The shock of discovering his wife in stark betrayal with a man he had welcomed under his roof. It was bound to destroy him. Judas, Nero, Ravan. My actions would be compared to those of history's most heinous villains . . . And the scandal of it all. Faint and corpse-like, I felt the blood slowly recede from my fingertips and toes.

CHAPTER TWENTY-TWO

Amma to the rescue

~

THE SHOCK OF discovering that my letter had gone missing led to an illness which lasted almost a week. The concerned faces of Mrs Pereira, Mrs Watanabe and the High Commission chauffeur, Gonzales, swam in and out through hot flashes of sleep and wakefulness. Once, I even imagined Kamala's cool, anxious palm pressed against my forehead.

Gonzales blamed the English water, a source of pneumonia-carrying germs, apparently. 'If I had my way,' I heard him say, 'all English taps would carry our Ganga water, one hundred per cent clean and holy.'

Mrs Pereira hinted at some deep, dark literary sorrow. I had been mumbling in my delirium, she insisted, and the name 'Seth' kept coming up. But Mrs Watanabe insisted it was the stress of fame, something she fully understood, what with the BBC and the Camden Black Women's Press hounding her for interviews.

'They want dirt, man,' she explained one afternoon, biting into some smelly fruit she had smuggled in from Tonga. 'They want me raped by missionaries, with babies at fourteen and cholera at seventeen. Tell us, tell us the whole dirty truth, they say.' She spat the seeds expertly out of the half-open window. 'And I say to them, you want me to lie? Look, there is Macdonald, twenty-three years together we have been now. True, he gets the itch in his pants sometimes, but then, hey, which man don't? I just look the other way. Plenty of other things to worry about, what with the cornbread factory shutting down thanks to some Chinky in Singapore who bakes cheaper bread. My four children are there. Got to help the good Lord in providing for them. But how can there be any poetry in all this, they say?'

Her voice flowed ceaselessly through the afternoon. 'Don't let small ups and down upset you, my little Indian friend. This is the price of being a good poet. As they say in Tonga, "Better a one-legged dog holding a bone than a two-legged man clutching an empty bowl."'

Only I knew better. Constantly throwing its hot, fevered image against my closed eyelids was the smiling, feline face of Naina, determinedly pulling me towards her, and in my ears was the quiet sound of Kamala weeping.

Was this what happened to all Indian women once let loose abroad? They couldn't wait to get their sari pleats off? And there, on the other hand, stood my Kamala, head respectfully covered as soon as an elderly male relative knocked at the door. Was this the Western threat Gandhiji had warned us about? Sharmila was right: I was no good at this English lifestyle. Who was I trying to fool with my fondness for English meat and wine and women wearing low-cut sleeveless blouses? Far better to belong to a Kamala stuck in medieval village ways than be with a Naina marching shamelessly immoral through the twentieth century.

I remembered a time when those typical Delhi December colds had forced me to lie in bed for a month. Kamala, with her own bare hands, had warmed an Ayurvedic concoction of dried neem leaves and cinnamon sticks over an open brazier. Wrapping it in a muslin cloth, she had gently pressed this over my chest through innumerable nights while reciting verses from the *Ramayana*.

I wept then for the wholesomeness of Rouse Avenue: the Friday-evening trips to India Gate, where Kamala insisted on setting free the Hanuman-shaped balloons, and where Feroze and I overate the *bhel-puri* and the *kwality* ice cream, our chins smeared with warm, melting vanilla, tongues still tingling to the tart, tamarind taste of the *bhel*. Amma would be busy reciting the names of all the unknown soldiers who had given their life for the Empire. Their names, finely etched, glowed softly through the blue-grey shadows of the early evening.

'His fever has broken. Look, he is crying again. Perhaps I shouldn't have sent that telegram so post haste.' The worried voice of Mrs Pereira broke through my tears. What telegram? Was Kamala being summoned to my bed like the angel Gabriel? But could I face her again so soon after my treachery?

'Please, Mrs Pereira.' I half rose weakly from the bed. 'Which ministering angel have you called?'

'No minister-vinister, you are only being a VIP to your mother, no one else. This is too much to cope up with, your fainting every second day. How am I to know which disease you are exporting from back home?

178

This is hotel, not hospital. Only hale and hearty types welcome under English skies.'

After this belligerent speech, Mrs Pereira tugged angrily at her cross and with one fierce glance left the room. She re-entered almost immediately.

'Here, something to cheer you up.'

A blue paper was waved close to my face. Her pink lipstick had rubbed off on her teeth, making her look like Kali, the goddess Kamala felt closest to during her feminine 'off' days.

'*Your SOS profoundly disturbing Stop I have not abandoned you Stop Am coming express fast Stop Funding no problem Stop Amma.*' So typical of my mother. Like a Walter Scott knight, she was rushing to the rescue.

Mrs Pereira, no doubt ashamed of her unkindness, reluctantly agreed to let me make another long-distance call. 'I suppose there is nothing purer than a mother's love. And I will charge you half-rate only, agreed, okay?'

It was Feroze who answered the phone, his slow 'hmms' and 'haas' irritating me no end.

'Feroze, tell Amma to cancel her trip. I am cured and on my feet again.'

How I hoped the urgency of my voice travelled sufficiently strongly on those long-distance lines. Feroze grunted something about KitKats and a comics list. This habit of half eating his sentences was something he had inherited from his mother. It annoyed me immensely, the way Kamala mumbleed and aborted a conversation in mid-flow, and this gift she had handed down to her son.

Amma, Feroze informed me, had already left for England on an Aeroflot flight with a free weekend stop-over and sightseeing tour of Moscow thrown in.

'But where the hell did she get the money from?' I shouted, thinking for a dreadful moment that she had sold our flat or pawned Kamala's wedding jewellery. Feroze burst into tears at this uncharacteristic chastisement and slammed the phone down.

There was only one explanation. Amma had, in desperation, helped herself to the Nehru Society funds, something she had vowed never to do. Would the Government ever forgive her? A warrant might be waiting for her in India, and she would end her grey-haired days in Tihar jail. What would her defence be? That only a mother's love could commit such a crime?

*

Gonzales was kind enough to collect Amma from the airport. 'Strictly for family's sake,' Mrs Pereira assured me. I learned then that Gonzales had recently resigned from his job. He was going to restart his life in, of all places, Portugal, where there was demand for honest, hard-working labour.

It was Amma who told me this, sitting by my side and gently rubbing Amritanjan balm (her remedy for life's every ailment) on my forehead.

It was good to have her in England. To see that small, determined frame darting around the room, shielded against the London cold by a crisp silk sari and sturdy Bata *chappals*. Before long she had negotiated a folding bed and breakfast for herself at no extra charge.

'I like your mother, Naidu,' Mrs Pereira said grudgingly, bringing in an extra hot-water bottle. 'She is real gutsy lady, true businesswoman like us Goanese, and there I am thinking she will be another weepy softie like you.'

Amma's arrival had the desired effect and I was soon sitting up in bed, my mind aflame with the next poetic project. This time it was to be on the bond uniting a mother and son.

'Amma, do you like this line? "From the shelter of my womb, I led you out."'

It was just like the cosy old days with Amma writing letters in one corner, Kamala away at the temple, jangling the bells, and the servant going out to get steaming chappatis and *dal makhani* from the street-corner tandoor.

'Something is worrying me about Kamala, Naidu.'

'Why? What could trouble you about such a simple soul?' I asked, thinking of Kamala's daily routine, as transparent as the muslin with which she polished her Ganeshas.

'No, no, just her loyalties have done a U-turn. You remember the Hare Krishna Centre that was opening near the washerwomen's *bustee?*'

I remembered it well. The building of the temple had created a lot of juicy gossip in the neighbourhood. It was made of Italian marble, and all the fixtures and fittings, from the doorknobs to the semi-precious stone crown on Krishna's head, had been imported from Oregon, USA.

'I'm glad she's started going there. I never liked that buttery priest from the Hanuman temple.'

Amma agreed with this but still insisted that a subtle sea change had come over her hitherto docile daughter-in-law. For instance, Kamala refused to tie Feroze's shoelaces for him any more, saying he was old enough to be responsible for putting on his own shoes.

'And then the next day my daily glass of milk fails to turn up. You know me, Kavi, I am hardly the nagging mother-in-law type, but when I gently ticked off Kamala for this, you know what she said?' Amma looked at me indignantly. 'That, this being Sunday, even daughter-in-laws needed a day of rest from daily drudgery. Mrs Basu is convinced that it is imported American values from that Krishna temple that are corrupting Kamala.'

To me, Amma's unnecessary concern about Kamala's religious shenanigans seemed hopelessly misplaced. Little did she know the duplicity of female nature. There was Naina, cheating on her husband left, right and centre, and here was my mother worrying about a loyalty shift from Hanuman to Krishna.

'Don't be too concerned about Kamala, Amma. Just be thankful she knows so little beyond her kitchen–temple world. You should see what other women, especially the westernised ones, are up to these days.'

Amma took my hands in hers and asked whether there was a female angle to my new mature outlook. 'Something is troubling you, son. This new wisdom is most uncharacteristic.' It was motherly intuition, she maintained. Nothing but womanly charms could have persuaded me to dilly-dally in England for so long and adopt so adult an attitude.

'But wouldn't you be shocked, Amma, if your married son made an emotional blunder with another? Would you still forgive him?' Surprise made me sit up straight and blurt it all out.

'Forgive? Why not? What dark ages are you living in, my son? To tell you the truth, as I am sure your dear, late father would agree, we never really gave your poetic heart a chance to bloom, did we? Even before you were properly standing on your own two feet, we were busy handcuffing you to the matrimonial mismatch of the century.' She ran her hand through my hair.

'Don't say that, Amma. Father was right. Kamala is, after all, a dutiful wife and mother, even though she may blank out at the mention of poetry. Perhaps we can persuade her to join the Open University?' I suggested, thinking of Mrs Watanabe's literary flowering.

'No, no. She is beyond repair. This was bound to happen.' Amma was obstinate in her denunciation. 'A handsome, gifted man like you, and these English ladies find Indian men irresistible – look at our own Nehruji and Edwina. So who is this English rose, then? Is she a literary type, too, a kindred spirit plucked from Oxford?'

I was on the verge of admitting my shameless treatment at the hands of Naina, and my worries about the missing letter, when Mrs Watanabe entered the room bearing an armful of violent red roses.

Amma's lips shrank into a thin, ruler-straight line as she busily put two and two together.

Mrs Watanabe threw us a bright, radiant smile. 'So this is the proud mother. Only an Indian or Tonganese mother would cross the seven seas to be by her child's dying side.'

This dramatic speech was followed by her smartly clicking open a delicate brocade fan, which she proceeded to wave near her open-necked yellow batik shirt.

'A gift from the Peking Women's Co-operative,' she explained to Amma, who was staring at her with ill-disguised curiosity. 'Guess what the inscription says?' Mrs Watanabe gazed at the hieroglyphics proudly. '"A hand of friendship from your Chinese sisters".'

Amma sat down suddenly in her chair, so forcefully that the springs squealed in protest. 'Don't tell me you are the lucky winner of this year's prize?'

'By God's grace, yes.' Mrs Watanabe flashed her teeth again and, leaning forward from the foot of the bed where she was sitting, squeezed Amma's hand understandingly. 'Let me tell you, as one mother to another, I understand. It must hurt, but your son will shine one day. The touching poems he writes, especially his Love Poems . . . He will win some day, or my name is not Joyous Emily Watanabe.'

Amma refused to accept Mrs Watanabe's sympathy and turning to me said, 'So much has changed since Nehru's time, Naidu. To think one day the English would be crowning a foreigner from nowhere.' She shook her head sadly. 'This England is declining at dog-speed.'

I looked at her wistfully. She had been in England less than twenty-four hours and disillusionment had already set in. She was bound to take Mrs Watanabe's victory personally, for ticking away beneath that Indian sari was a strawberries-and-cream heart.

Mrs Watanabe had listened to Amma's words attentively. The fan was clicked shut and she reclined on the bed in a most familiar fashion. From where I lay, I could even catch a glimpse of a bra strap made of some colourful lacy material.

'Your mother, she has been in England before? She sounds a world-wise tourist.' Mrs Watanabe looked at me for guidance.

'One can travel through the mind, you know, through books, music, et cetera. We Indians tend to be quite naturally inclined that way. Africa being such a distant continent, you couldn't possibly know all this,' Amma said sarcastically, deliberately misplacing Tonga on the world map.

I had never seen this knife-edge side to Amma before. There she was, slicing Mrs Watanabe like an onion, quite forgetting all her Nehruvian ideals of universal love and brotherhood.

Not to be outdone, Mrs Watanabe rolled up her sparring sleeves. 'Oh, Tonga may be a distant dot in the ocean, all right, Mother' – Amma frowned at the title – 'but a Tonganese heart is very close to the stars.'

She paused to consider what she had said, then beamed. 'I like that. I will put it in my next poem, Naidu. In fact, guess what?' The ample bosom was lowered confidentially over me as she zoomed in on my face. 'I might even propose it as a rewording of our national anthem to the Prime Minister.'

'But what about your work in the chicken factory?' asked Amma. 'My son here happens to be a full-time poet.'

'Cornbread, not chicken,' Mrs Watanabe corrected her cheerfully. 'And what does it matter, full or part? I tell you, it is when the dark clouds inside me begin to sing that a pen appears as if by magic in my hand. Anyway, I must be going now. Another book signing in Camden.'

Mrs Watanabe kissed me wetly on both cheeks, winked twice, and, with a whispered 'The second kiss for your high moral code', left the room with an energetic wave.

No sooner had the door shut than Amma pounced on me. 'So, are you hoping her success rubs off on you? This is your English Juliet? Your English rose? This is the romantic muse you left poor old Kamala for? No shame, kissing you in front of your own mother. These tribals have no morals. No wonder your wife and your old sickly mother have been thrown out of the window.'

Before I could defend Mrs Watanabe's reputation and clear the confusion, the door opened again and Mrs Pereira came in. She stood near the window, smelling Mrs Watanabe's roses in a most irritating way. The light from the window caught her peach dress, making it transparent. For some obscure reason, I thought of Matthew Joseph.

'How is your student friend from Madgaon doing?' I asked as a way of deflecting attention from the roses. Amma had put on her reading spectacles and was examining the accompanying note.

'What can students be doing these days? Only reading, writing and minding their own business.' Mrs Pereira giggled, one hand flying girlishly up to her mouth. This was called puppy love. Never had Kamala or even Naina laughed in this manner.

'Jawahar.' Amma rarely addressed me by my forgotten name. 'This message with the flowers, it is most mysterious. What on earth does that *junglee* woman mean?'

Mrs Pereira snatched the note from Amma's hand and read it out: '"My friend, a rod in use will never be abused. Keep yours thumping away."'

After some intense soul-searching, I decided against telling Amma about Naina. Enlightened as she was, her childish behaviour regarding Mrs Watanabe had convinced me that my romantic bruising at the hands of a married lady a good many years my senior would not be viewed in the right light.

'Amma, forget your meeting with Mr Mistry. These highly placed people are so busy, you know.' I hoped to dissuade her, still fearful of what impact my missing letter was having on Mr Mistry.

'But you have spoken so highly of them, Naidu. I really must pay my respects now that I am here.'

Fortunately, this potential time bomb would have to be postponed as both Mr Mistry and Naina were away in the Caribbean attending a Non-aligned Conference on child labour in the carpet industry.

*

'There is some hanky-panky going on between those two,' Amma announced one morning. It seemed she had seen Mrs Pereira emerging from Matthew Joseph's room at dawn, when she herself, still fighting Indian Standard Time and not wishing to disturb me, was walking in the lobby.

'What hanky-panky, Amma? She just mothers him, that's all; he is far from home.' I didn't want Amma's upright morals corrupted so soon.

'What sort of mothering is this that takes place only at night?' she snorted. 'I have my eye trained on them. This is the third morning she comes out, wearing only a cheap silky nighty. Why does she have to dress like one of those Anglo-Indian vamps in our Hindi movies?'

CHAPTER TWENTY-THREE

A suburban interlude

⌒

WHILE WAITING FOR my health to make a total recovery before our return to India, Amma decided to visit an old schoolfriend of hers, one Mrs Rama Joshi, whose husband had come to England in the early Sixties. So caught up was I in the turns and twists of my own problems that I had forgotten to contact her, despite Amma's strict instructions to do so.

'Do visit her, Naidu. It will be like a home away from home for you, not that we were particularly close in school. All she ever wanted was to move to England with a husband who would make her live like a queen. Still, her mother made the most wonderful mouth-melting *dhoklas*.'

Mrs Joshi lived in a part of London that even Mrs Pereira couldn't locate on her map of the centre. Some sixth sense had warned Mrs Pereira that Amma was aware of her nocturnal deeds and she now avoided us in a nervous, clumsy way, pleading a headache or her accounts as an excuse whenever we invited her to share our afternoon cup of tea.

We eventually found Mrs Joshi's house way out in west London, in a long road occupied by a row of identical homes. Large jumbo jet planes periodically swooped overhead, drowning our conversation. Amma looked around with disapproval, delicately lifting the hem of her sari over some fly-away newspapers lying on the pavement.

'Much has changed since Nehruji's time,' she sighed, ringing the bell of number fifty-two Leigh Gate Road.

'What if she's out? You should have let me telephone first,' I said angrily, thinking of our countless changes of train.

'She will be in. After all, Rama must be only a full-time housewife.'

At that moment, an elderly Indian lady approached the house. Dressed in a navy-blue tracksuit, her hair tied back in an untidy grey ponytail, she was roughly Amma's age. A large maroon *bindi* covered most of her forehead.

I ran to help with the two large shopping bags she was carrying. 'You must be Rama Auntie. I have heard so much about you from Amma.'

Puzzled, she looked at me and then at Amma, who was staring at her with a curious expression. The maroon *bindi* lifted in surprise and an uncertain smile broke the severity of her face.

'Shobha, can it really be you?' Only rarely did I hear Amma addressed by her first name. I had forgotten how musical it sounded.

Auntie Rama's house was in a sorry state. I think we in Rouse Avenue boasted better material standards with our large airy verandas and profusion of flower-pots. A large television dominated the drawing room, where the sofas and the carpet were a faded patchy brown. Peach-coloured curtains firmly shut out the daylight, and I could barely make out a large holiday picture, taken at the seaside, of a much younger Auntie Rama wearing large sunglasses and holding five scowling small boys. Hung next to it on the wall was a Gujerati calendar on which certain dates had been heavily circled in red ink.

Amma enquired about the children over some savoury Gujerati *sev* and masala tea. An embarrassed laugh followed each query, but Amma kept pressing in her direct manner.

'So, you are a poet, *beta*,' said Mrs Joshi, skilfully turning the conversation. 'So impressive, government-paid trip to England. We always said Shobha would go far.'

Amma beamed at the compliment and took the opportunity to inform her friend of the recent activities of the Nehru Society.

Auntie Rama listened politely, a vague smile fixed on her face. Her eyes from time to time darted over to the cuckoo clock hung over the television set. Embarrassed, no doubt, by her English attire, she had draped a type of *chunni* over her shoulder, and the light chiffon material contrasted starkly with the rough, masculine cut of her tracksuit.

'And Joshiji must be hard at work in the office. The Transport Ministry, isn't it, or has he retired?'

Before Auntie Rama could reply, the door opened and a wild-looking English girl entered the room and flung herself into a chair. She reminded me of a Shakespearean creature from *The Tempest*, with her untidy short hair, flimsy skirt and mud-stained shoes. Her black socks ended just below the knee and the round, white balls of her knees looked back defiantly at us

190

from where she sat. Amma looked at Auntie Rama, who looked at the carpet. The girl, unconcerned by this silent exchanging of looks, sat there flicking through a television magazine.

Eventually, with some effort, Auntie Rama said, 'This is Anita, my eldest daughter-in-law. You remember Ramesh? This is his wife.'

'So this is the eldest *bahu*.' Amma needed to say no more.

Anita's entrance seemed to have thrown a cloud over Auntie Rama. Her voice became high-pitched and brittle as she fretted over our lunch arrangements.

Amma politely refused the half-hearted invitation to stay for some cheese and onion pie from the local chip shop, and we took our leave.

'So much for living like a queen! Is this what she left India for?' Amma exclaimed angrily as soon as the front door closed behind us. 'You noticed there was no mention of what her sons did. I bet they are good-for-nothing train conductors or postmen. And look at that Anita. English girls are not what they used to be, no blushing roses like our Edwina was.' Amma took my hand and held it tightly all the way to the station.

'Thank God I came when I did, or I could so easily have lost you to all this.' The sweep of her arm took in the cold, deserted railway platform with its hoardings of bright sunshine holidays, the stationmaster, an Indian like us, hunched over a newspaper in his booth, and the two teenage English boys wearing earrings, arguing quietly and furiously near the Gents' toilet.

CHAPTER TWENTY-FOUR

Do all gods have feet of clay?

❧

'A TEARFUL FEMALE admirer is calling,' Mrs Pereira informed me on that fateful day.

I took the call with trepidation: perhaps it was a ransom demand for my vanished letter?

An excited English voice poured into my ear. 'Mr Naidu, I need to see you urgently. You don't know me, but I am Cordelia Cardigan, special assistant to the chief editor at Ostrich.'

'Ostrich?' My mind blanked out for a moment as I thought of Delhi zoo. 'As in the bird?'

'As in the publishers. Mr Naidu, I need to see you immediately,' the voice repeated impatiently.

We arranged to meet at a French coffee house in Soho where Miss Cardigan insisted they baked the best baguettes this side of Paris.

'A most unsavoury part of London it is,' Mrs Pereira said when I asked for directions. 'Full of – she lowered her eyebrows delicately – 'ladies of the night servicing in broad daylight. It is walkable from here but be careful not to trip. You poets are all busy cutting the same cloth. Why, there was that scoundrel Byron chasing Empress Josephine.' She became quite fierce in her denunciation.

Much as I would have liked Amma to accompany me to this rendezvous, after some deliberation we decided against it. Miss Cardigan, we felt, might not be able to unburden herself in the presence of an unknown third party.

Mrs Pereira was right: Soho was just like a seedier version of old Delhi. Most of the shops brazenly advertised female flesh, and unshaven men loitered in the doorways, looking aimless and unclean. Rubbish overflowed from the bins in cheerful abandon. A tramp carefully urinating into a beer bottle swore at me when I asked him for directions. At least Amma had been spared these modern Western sights.

In the coffee house, an attractive girl with red hair sat warming her hands round a large coffee cup. Sober black spectacles contrasted pleasantly with the whiteness of her cheeks, which glowed gently in the afternoon light. Dotting her very long, very visible legs was a charming sprinkling of freckles.

I recognised Miss Cardigan immediately. She was the girl I had seen with Seth the day of my lunch with Mrs Watanabe. My heart did a somersault on seeing her warm smile. I was at last living the life of a cosmopolitan Bohemian. If only Binoy or Sharmila could see me now, alone in the company of a fine young Englishwoman.

'How loyal you are to your clan, Miss Cardigan.' I pointed to the tiny Scottish kilt she was wearing. 'It is so good to see young girls upholding the traditions in these modern times.'

Miss Cardigan, despite her red-rimmed eyes, gave a girlish giggle. 'Actually, I'm Australian, Mr Naidu, from Perth. Never set foot in Scotland. The kilt is the nearest I've ever been to a glen.' That giggle again.

193

Suddenly her bright blue eyes clouded over and, even though we were the only occupants of the coffee house, she lowered her voice. 'Mr Naidu, I know we haven't met before, but I must tell you that something terrible has come up. There are scores I wish to settle and only you can help me do it.'

Could it be love? How sensitive these Western women were. Somehow, somewhere, she had read my poems and fallen in love. But after the fiasco with Naina I was in no mood to commit further misdemeanours with unknown women. However, before I could gently dissuade her from seeking my affections and inform her of my marital status, she had uttered the dreaded word 'Seth'. That scoundrel managed to sneak into every situation, directly or indirectly.

'I have discovered something terrible about him and I need your advice.'

I leaned forward, excitement rushing through my veins.

The old woman standing behind the pastry counter came over to take my order. Despite Miss Cardigan's protests, I ordered a milky tea.

'But the coffee here is excellent, you really ought to try it.'

I waved aside her argument. 'I find your Nescafé coffee too strong. Anyway, before you start making damaging revelations, may I remind you, Miss Cardigan, that as fellow poets Seth and I are kindred spirits. Competitors, yes, but soulmates none the less. Any advice I give you will therefore be strictly biased in his favour.'

Miss Cardigan looked at me in a strange, assessing, almost pitying way and reached thoughtfully into her bag for a cigarette. 'If only you knew what he thinks of you – but that shouldn't matter. Listen, do you remember that poem of Seth's "Shout after me No"?'

I nodded. Remember? How could I forget. The damn poem, published a few years back, had created a global sensation, aided by Seth's smooth public-relations machinery. Hailed as an expression of Third World anger, it had been adopted as a freedom song by the South African anti-apartheid movement. In the Soviet Union it had picked up the Trotsky Prize for Global Understanding, while in India no less a person than the Chief Minister of Kashmir had called for it to be translated into all the vernacular languages.

'Of course I know the poem, Miss Cardigan. Like it or not, it is part of our national consciousness.' And I proceeded to recite it from memory.

> ' "The face in the mirror shouts No.
> No to centuries of being ground to dust,
> No to indignities of a handcuffed soul.
> A nation of dwarfs have we become,
> Marching to the beat of a foreigner's drum,
> Pleading for a glimpse of a borrowed tomorrow.
> No more. No more. The shadow fallen to its knee.
> The face in the mirror shouts No." '

In spite of myself, the forceful delivery quite stirred me, and I asked for some water.

'Moving words, you will agree, Miss Cardigan. Credit where credit's due.'

'Moving or not moving, this is the original,' Miss Cardigan said impatiently and, reaching into her sack-like bag, she took out a crumpled little paperback and handed it to me.

It was in a foreign language; I stared blankly at the print. 'What do you mean, original? Seth's mother tongue is English, just like mine.'

'Don't you understand?' She took my hand and shook it excitedly. 'It isn't Seth's work at all. He copied it word for word from this Mr Burman, a retired school-teacher from Darjeeling.'

The blood halted in my veins. I felt faint, but suspicion made me cautious. This was Cold War, an American conspiracy to set me up against a fellow writer. Seth was well known to have Soviet sympathies.

'Just who has sent you, Miss Cardigan, and why are you hell-bent on spoiling a good Indian's name?'

The coffee shop was full now and my raised voice attracted some attention.

'You're right. I need to bring you up to date.' Miss Cardigan vigorously stirred some more sugar into her half-empty cup. 'You know Seth's been a star writer with Ostrich for a good many years now? We became "close friends" – I mean very close.'

I winced at her words. Was no woman safe from that lascivious hand?

'And then things began to turn sour. Particularly this time.' Miss Cardigan wiped a tear from her cheek.

I pressed her hand sympathetically. This was obviously nothing but a lovers' tiff. 'Look, if you want me to play the go-between, I will. Is there a message you want me to carry to him? Maybe I could pen a poem to bring him back to you?'

Miss Cardigan laughed so hard that she almost fell off her chair. 'You still don't get the message, Naidu, do you? It's bloody revenge I want, not some namby-pamby reunion! How do you think I felt, walking in on them in *my* bed in *my* flat, her shameless body writhing in front of me? And you know what the bastard said? "Cordelia, darling, my highway rose, this will be most educational for our future life together. A representative from the land of the *Kama Sutra* to give you some hands-on training,"' Miss Cardigan imitated Seth's cultivated tones perfectly.

But who was the sinning third party? Bound to be an Indian, since the *Kama Sutra* was involved. Could it be . . . ? I shook my head firmly. No, not Naina. Seth couldn't stand her. Our conversation in the park was testimony to that.

Miss Cardigan was still waiting for my reaction. Hot colour rising to her cheeks turned them a most pleasing shade, the colour of apples from Simla.

'Well?' Perplexed, I looked at her. 'What is there to do? Maybe he has transferred his affections. Such things do happen – remember *Gone with the Wind.'*

'Nobody transfers their affections from Cordelia Cardigan just like that,' she replied menacingly. 'That swine needs to be taught a lesson, and you'll be the one doing the teaching. You must meet Seth and tell him his plagiarising days are over. That shameless shit will be exposed to the world unless he agrees to our terms. After all, we have the proof.' Miss Cardigan waved the incriminating book gaily.

'But how do you know about this book, and what drastic terms are you proposing?' I was still suspicious and cautious.

'Oh, it was easy. Like all men, that shit-hole loves to hear his own voice singing, especially after a good bonk. And it all came spilling out then. He thought I'd be impressed by his cleverness, duping a poor simpleton from the mountains.'

What an unfortunate choice of words, so much at variance with Miss Cardigan's delicate Scottish looks.

'But why don't you do this revenging yourself? Just report him to your boss at Ostrich. Why involve me?'

I glanced at my watch. The British Museum would be closing in an hour, and I had promised Amma a visit to the Chinese pottery department.

'Because coming from you, all this will hurt the bastard much, much more. The supposedly ball-less twopenny poet suddenly topples the god from his pedestal!'

'Really, Miss Cardigan, there is no need to get personal. It is not twopenny verse I am writing. Whatever you may think of my poetry, the world happens to hold it in considerable esteem.'

I got up to leave, but surprisingly strong arms pinned me back into my seat.

'Don't get me wrong. I'm sorry, I didn't mean to offend you. I was merely quoting Seth. You see, he simply can't stand you. What did he call you the other day . . . ?' Miss Cardigan scratched her chin. Memory triumphantly returned. 'Ah, yes, a freeloading foetus brain.'

For the second time that day, the blood halted in my veins. Miss Cardigan, noticing my hurt expression, recommended sharing a ham and cheese baguette (despite tragic events in her life, she maintained a healthy appetite).

She refused to say any more until the baguette arrived. Then, 'I'm going to ring Seth,' she said, taking out an important-looking black book.

'Stop! Please stop. What are you going to say?' Alarmed, I caught her hand.

'Dead simple, really. I'll suggest a meeting between you and him. We'll threaten to expose him unless . . .' She paused dramatically and bit sharply into her half of the baguette.

'Unless?' I prompted.

After thoroughly chewing the last bite of crunchy lettuce, she continued, 'Unless he pushes your cause with Peterson, makes sure you get a place in the Commonwealth anthology that Ostrich is bringing out. That more than anything else should kill him.' She sat back, smiling.

*

The telephone call to Seth yielded no reply and Miss Cardigan, convinced that hanky-panky was being conducted once again in her flat, persuaded me to accompany her there. It was located in Islington, an avant-garde part of London, Miss Cardigan informed me, and the building reminded me vaguely of Father O'Brian's Centre for Battered Women. The corridor to her flat held the same musty smell of people wearing too many unwashed sweaters. We stopped outside a chipped green door, and Miss Cardigan curled her delicate Scottish nose theatrically.

'I was right! The bastard's here again. That's his aftershave all right.'

How much in tune with their environment these Western women were. As for Kamala, her nose was dead to every smell but sandalwood incense and *pakoras* frying.

We could have been in a Shakespearean drama. This was a female Othello turning the door handle softly on her male Desdemona. Sprawled on Miss Cardigan's bed like a sunning lion would be a naked Seth, lolling around with some exotic woman. But then again, did I really want to see him in that vulnerable position?

'Stop, Miss Cardigan. I am sorry, I cannot accompany you inside. It is not a very gentlemanly or dignified thing to do.'

'Do you think he's being a gentleman in my bed right now?' Miss Cardigan replied scornfully, flinging open the door.

'I promise to meet him for the sake of poetry, but catch him like this I just can't, Miss Cardigan.'

I turned and fled, intent on discussing the new turn of events with Amma.

While crossing the road, I was almost run over by a familiar-looking car trying to find parking opposite Miss Cordelia's building. It was Gonzales, waving to me amiably.

CHAPTER TWENTY-FIVE

The confrontation

〜

MISS CARDIGAN'S APPEARANCE in my life had suddenly turned everything topsy and turvy. Three possible scenarios could now take place, and I mulled over them as I set off for the dreaded meeting, to be held ironically in St James's Park, where just a few weeks back Seth and I had exchanged opinions as equals.

Scenario One would have a guilty, contrite Seth falling at my feet, begging forgiveness. He would confess that it was my poetic style he was hoping to emulate all along and would entreat me to be his literary mentor. This possibility sounded far-fetched even to me and I immediately dismissed it.

Scenario Two would result in Seth admitting his misdemeanour in a quiet, dignified way, and treating me as an equal by requesting advice on how to rectify the situation. In appreciation of my moral superiority, he would suggest bringing out a celebratory volume of my most recent works at his own expense. He also promised to introduce me to his literary jet-set friends and coterie of desirable women.

The third and final scenario had Seth turning up late for the rendezvous, and reducing me to a pathetic figure of ridicule by pointing out all the flaws in my personality. I would be roughly punched to the ground as a parting gesture.

I wavered between the last two versions while making my way to the appointment.

What a memorable evening it was, the park sliced into two neat slivers of light and dark by the setting sun. The weeping willow beneath which I stood waiting for Seth seemed lit by an inner fire, every vein of its lean-fingered leaves strangely alive. Occasional hurrying feet or the gentle swish of a woman's skirt broke the evening quiet.

Seth's expensive alligator shoes finally approached, an hour late, the pebbles on the footpath parting like biblical waves before his feet. Panic seized me. The meeting might easily turn ugly.

I remembered my earlier conversation with his ex-lady-love.

'Please, Miss Cardigan, forget all this bitterness, forget . . . forgive. Let the stream of life flow on.'

'Hey, don't do a Gandhi on me now! And after what you have heard. You must be crazy.' The venom in her voice had been like a slap. 'This is the only way to shrink his balls to size.'

If Seth was furious to see me, he did not show it. One eyebrow arched a little as he leaned forward to light a cigarette.

'You look a bit uptight, Naidu. What is it? English food not agreeing with you? Or can it be brooding over failures past, present and future?'

Refusing to be drawn into this childish banter, I stepped forward and wordlessly handed him Mr Burman's book.

Seth flicked through the pages carelessly. 'Didn't know you were into the vernacular, Naidu. I suppose your grasp of the English language was never that strong. Too many metaphors and similes.'

'It is not my poetic achievements but yours we are discussing, Seth.' I snatched the book from him and opened it at the offending page. 'Recognise this? Roughly translated, it means "Shout after me No."'

Seth listened quietly as I spelled out, as precisely as I could, the extent to which his plagiarism had fouled the name of literature. He continued smoking, one arm insolently flung along the bench on which he had suddenly sat down.

'You have brought shame to the name of poetry, Mr Seth' (I used the formal address as a rebuke). 'A man of your integrity and standing, how could you steal another man's verse? Never again will Indian poets be revered after this shameful episode. And that poor Mr Burman. Little does he know, sitting in his classroom in Darjeeling, that he's been robbed of recognition by none other than our national poet laureate. This is a betrayal worthy of Judas.'

Emotion prevented me from speaking further and I reached for my handkerchief. Tomorrow it might be my own verse Seth was stealthily stealing.

To my utter amazement, instead of hanging his head in shame, Seth jumped up from the bench and walked round me, clapping loudly in appreciation.

'Bravo, bravo! A born orator – Mark Antony reborn. Now cut the crap, Naidu, and tell me the real motive behind this self-righteous chest beating, you self-seeking worm,' he muttered almost under his breath, coming closer and looking down at me from his great height. So near was he that I could make out the grey hairs in his nostrils and the thin noble-looking blue vein lightly throbbing on his forehead.

'A full written apology, no less. I want you to write to all the major publications, confessing your crime, and to redirect your medals and the earnings from that poem to Mr Burman's humble doorstep in Darjeeling.'

'Wait a minute, Naidu, we want something more.' Just then, as if in an Agatha Christie novel, the aggrieved figure of Miss Cardigan, dressed again in the minuscule Scottish kilt, materialised from behind a bush. There she stood facing Seth, hands resting on her hips in true Amazon warrior fashion. Only the slight trembling of her lower lip betrayed the inner turmoil she was going through.

'My highway rose! I should have guessed. But what a delicious surprise. Look, you're chilled to the bone. Let me.' Going over to Miss Cardigan, an unruffled Seth gallantly removed his jacket, draped it over her shoulders, and gently led her to the bench.

'There's something more, Seth,' she continued, ignoring his chivalrous gesture. 'We want you to talk Peterson into publishing Naidu's poems in the Commonwealth anthology and arranging a few poetry readings for him, here in England. Otherwise, this' – taking Mr Burman's book from me, she waved it like a pirate's flag – 'will find its way to Peterson's desk.'

I looked at her in admiration. So carried away was I by the enormity of Seth's crime against literature that I had quite forgotten to further my own cause.

Nevertheless, I wished the meeting did not have to take on quite such an ugly note. Seth, hitherto cool and collected, turned furious at Miss Cardigan's unreasonable demand.

I tried to placate him. 'Listen.' I grabbed his sleeve. 'The germ of a poem has formed inside me that captures our predicament. Listen.' And I recited:

> 'You and I have both
> Sipped nectar
> From the same bowl,
> The bowl called poetry.
> You used this nectar to paint the dark,
> I to turn the ugliness bright.
> Bright or dark, what matters in the end
> Is standing thirsty, side by side,
> Equals in all but name.'

'And you expect me to promote that kind of buffoonery at Ostrich?' Seth demanded, running an agitated hand through his thick head of hair. 'But, my highway rose, listen.'

He took Miss Cardigan to one side so that they were partially obscured by a large purple-flowered bush whose name I did not know. Trying to be discreet, I kept my head firmly down, mournfully counting the pebbles round my feet. Random violent phrases like 'scum of humanity' and 'tired prick' floated to me on the gentle evening air. And then, as abruptly as she had come, Cordelia left in a flurry of tears, pressing Seth's silk handkerchief against her mouth.

Seth emerged from behind the bush, biting his lower lip in an unusual show of vulnerability, I was quick to note.

'So, you unscrupulous parasite,' he sneered, 'you have

pulled it off again. Didn't one vanity publication satisfy your ego? Now you want me to promote your third-rate adolescent trash – using a woman's broken heart to exploit the situation, too.' He shook his head pityingly at me and took his leave, the pebbles parting once again to smooth his way.

His vicious last words stunned me. Personal attacks on my physical stature or looks I could take, but this slight on my character and poetry I was not prepared to bear. Was Seth correct? Was I truly so unscrupulous that I was ready to stoop to any means to see my poetry published? There seemed something intrinsically wrong in that.

Slowly I walked back to the hotel, feeling anything but victorious, oblivious of the sights and sounds of London bustling around me, bright, cheerful ribbons of light carrying people to evenings filled with laughter and loving.

Each pearl I take out,
One by one,
Stringing the sky with words of hope.
At night, I return each pearl to the shell.
Only I know its precious worth.

CHAPTER TWENTY-SIX

An unexpected arrival

SETH'S BITTER WORDS rankled, especially at night when, heavy-lidded yet unable to sleep, like a Dostoyevsky hero, I created imaginary cracks in the ceiling and spelled out Seth's snarling words.

'Really, Cordelia, it's too much. I accept everything, but to promote this Naidu would be a form of literary suicide. Don't you understand? The chap is denser than a Dickensian fog. He's a minor clerk who happens to dabble in poetry in his free time and wangled, God knows how, a trip here. Every street in Delhi is littered with "poets" like him.'

My downcast demeanour over the next few days galvanised Amma into taking action, and I returned from the British Museum one afternoon to find her huddled deep in conversation with Miss Cardigan, of all people. What an incongruous pair they made. Amma's deep-bordered Mysore silk sari was wrapped tightly round her small, bird-like frame, and her rapidly thinning hair was coiled neatly into a bun on top of her head – a style, she never ceased reminding me, much favoured by Mrs Bandaranaike, the Prime Minister of Ceylon. Sitting beside her, Cordelia Cardigan looked like a friendly female Gulliver, innocently underdressed, with acres of vulnerable-looking pale flesh exposed to the world.

'Your mum and I,' reported Miss Cardigan in a smug, I-knew-better-all-along tone, 'have put our heads together and come up trumps. I shouldn't have wasted time talking to you Naidu, she's much more daring.'

'And what have the two witches been brewing this time?' I enquired, indulging them by bantering. I was in a good mood, for Naina was still in hibernation on some Caribbean island, and within the dark, brooding shelves of the Manuscript Department of the British Museum I had stumbled across an unpublished poem of Tennyson's which bore a striking resemblance to one of my own. Whatever Seth might think, it was I, not he, who was continuing the lineage of classical English poetry.

Amma smiled as though *laddus* wouldn't melt in her mouth. 'Wait and see, Naidu. That serpent Seth will not know what has hit him. His days in the literary hall of fame are numbered. This gracious young lady' – here Amma pressed Miss Cardigan's hand warmly – 'has explained all to me, and between the two of us we have hatched the most amazing, sinister plan.'

They giggled like two schoolgirls caught mooning over the photograph of a matinee idol like Amitabh Bacchan.

*

Mr Dev Kant Jha Burman, MA Hons. in Literature from Kohima University, Head Teacher in English at the Tenzing Bhimpu High School for Girls in

Darjeeling, arrived on the Air India flight from Calcutta.

I took an immediate liking to him. DJ, as he implored us to call him, was a short, stocky man of anywhere between forty and fifty. He had a razor-sharp, thin moustache, trimmed in the style of Clark Gable. His mouth, bleached pale by the vigorous winters of Darjeeling, constantly broke into an eager, pleasing smile. Much to my amazement, he spoke respectable English, with the lilt of the Himalayas in his voice.

Miss Cardigan, as his official sponsor in England, took him under her wing. He was to board with her while she and Amma concocted ways of thrusting him into the limelight.

'Shout after me No', DJ informed us solemnly over what had become an obligatory shared cup of afternoon tea, was conceived originally as an underground protest song for the Bodo Separatist Movement. Seth, while holidaying in Darjeeling with his current paramour, had chanced to hear it recited at a tea planter's cocktail party. He had immediately arranged a meeting with Burman, to discuss its translation into both Hindi and English.

'How was I to know that the respected *babu* had ulterior motives in his heart?' Burman remarked sadly, eyes clouding with sorrow, yet those pale, thin lips breaking into a smile from sheer force of habit.

'And he milked it for all it was worth, didn't he, while you were busy yodelling in the Himalayas?' Cordelia Cardigan exclaimed grimly, plucking a loose thread from my bedspread.

My room functioned as a sort of clandestine meeting place in which all the subversives assembled after sunset. Amma functioned as a moderator, calming us down when the tirades against Seth threatened to get out of hand.

We each of us had our own grievance. I related the humiliation I had suffered at that poet's gathering, so many years ago. Cordelia described how Seth used to boast of his amorous conquests, three hundred and fifty of them to be precise, even while professing undying love for her. It was DJ's story, however, which tugged the hardest at the heartstrings.

'Most gentlemanly he was,' Burman told us in his halting, Himalayan lilt. 'Gave me his personal word of honour. "Burman, I will make sure your epic poem earns the fame it deserves."'

There was something special about our comradely evenings, a flavour I appreciated only much later. The way the sinking sun flooded the room, lighting up Cordelia's freckles like scattered, splintered jewels. The way DJ would suddenly, inexplicably, burst into a plaintive folk song, his voice as undulating as the mountains he'd left behind. And above all Amma, flitting constantly between my room and the tea-making facilities in the hotel lobby, bearing flasks of cardamom-shot tea to fortify our spirits.

Through all these evenings, though, I sat tense with apprehension. There was a blurring of right and wrong. Seth had in his own inimitable way hurt each one of us, but to conspire against him like this was something I could not entirely condone in my heart.

*

Sooner than I had anticipated, our opportunity arrived. The occasion was a prestigious poetry reading at none

210

other than Blackwater's bookshop – a venerable institution linked to both Oxford and Cambridge. Peterson, the Ostrich editor, was to be present, and Seth would introduce some of the Commonwealth poets and read a few of his own choice verses; 'Shout after me No' was to be one of them.

Miss Cardigan could barely contain her excitement as she delivered the good news. 'It is ultra hush-hush, the whole plan. I think he's worried sick you might hijack the event.'

That night I penned a poem.

The shadows gather.
The storm clouds beckon.
The fight between right and wrong,
Just and unjust, is about to commence.
May the one whose heart is purer than snow
Be the one to greet the dawn.

CHAPTER TWENTY-SEVEN

A small man from a small village

⌐⌐

SETH WAS ALREADY there in the bookshop, cutting a dignified figure against a shelf of leather-bound tomes. He frowned when he saw me, and quickly went over to DJ. For some reason Seth insisted on speaking to him in a slow, very basic way, often gesticulating to illustrate a point. DJ, I was glad to note, refused the condescending bait and answered all observations and queries regarding his sudden arrival in England and the coldness of the British weather in perfect English.

Seth started his speech: 'Ladies and gentlemen . . .'

Even though I was only part of the audience, a sudden stage nervousness overtook me and I kept my eyes resolutely fixed on the shelf containing works of Imperial History. Despite a long and some might say distinguished career in writing, it was not often that I was called upon to attend poetry readings with such a sinister bent to them. The significance of the moment was not lost on me, or for that matter on Amma, who, perched on a little stepladder at the side of the room, kept giving me encouraging nods.

As Seth meandered on about the contribution to English writing of the non-English, some of the more restless listeners strolled over to a table where liquid refreshment was being provided by an excited Miss Cardigan. A middle-aged man in a smart navy double-breasted blazer began loudly arguing about something with two rather plain ladies who were noisily sipping from little plastic cups held tightly against their flat chests.

All this general hullabaloo died down the moment Mrs Watanabe opened her mouth. She more than made up for the substandard quality of her verse by an electric stage presence. There was much pointing of fingers and banging of the table, her arms moving like graceful ebony snakes through the pink bell-shaped sleeves of her native dress, a straight-from-the-heart delivery which brought loud claps of appreciation. Though I was not so keen on her style of bombastic verse, two particular lines struck a chord, bringing back bitter-sweet memories:

'The lightning that ran from your hand to mine,
The brush of your evening beard against my secret skin.'

It was refreshing to hear such fine sentiments emerging from such a plump, wholesome being.

So taken were people by Mrs Watanabe's poetry that their attention rapidly dwindled once the other poets took the floor, even though Seth took great pains over introducing them all, emphasising their deprived, unemployed backgrounds and the suffering that characterised their poetry.

'Naidu, now is the time. Go and seize the moment,' Amma kept hissing into my ear.

Irritated by her insistence, I edged behind a bookshelf.

'All right, then, let me do it my way.' And right before my astonished eyes, Amma swiftly walked to the centre of the room, sparrow-like in her pale blue sari. She firmly pushed Seth to one side and began to speak.

'Ladies and gentlemen, brothers and sisters, may I introduce you to the one star that did not shine today, the one true voice who, through a cruel twist of human deceit, was denied his rightful place in the poetic hall of fame being celebrated today.'

She looked around at her spellbound audience and, satisfied by the response, continued, 'Ladies and gentlemen, I speak of a humble schoolteacher who stands anonymous and unrecognised among you today. He has crossed seven seas and seven mountains, not for fame or glory but only in the cause of fair play. Please welcome Mr D. J. Burman with an open heart.'

'Burman, Burman . . .' The two plain women took up the chant as though he were a cricketing celebrity, a Sunil Gavaskar coming home with the trophy.

Taken aback by the unexpectedly warm welcome, Burman reluctantly allowed himself to be pushed centre stage by a beaming Amma. Mopping his brow, his trademark Nepali fur hat slightly askew, he looked lost and out of place, like a mountain goat caught in the headlights of an interstate truck. His small, bead-like eyes ran over the faces surrounding him; the mouth beneath the razor-sharp moustache trembled and wavered. Suddenly bowing his head in utter humility, hands folded gracefully, Burman spoke, intermingling his English with Hindi phrases. *'Prabhu ki kripa se*, by the grace of God, I am in front of all you good people. A small man from a small village. Many, many years ago I wrote a poem describing the hopes of my people. Nothing fancy, just the pain of a simple heart put on paper. Then one day, this smart sahib from Delhi comes.' He pointed at Seth. 'This smart sahib with his beautiful English and beautiful clothes took an immediate interest in my poem and kindly agreed to arrange its translation and publication.' Overcome by emotion, Burman swallowed once or twice.

'The years passed and my hair turned to grey. I started teaching class ten about the daffodils of Sir Wordsworth and thought no more of my own humble poem. Then one day a telegram arrives from this fine English lady here.'

A dozen heads turned to where Cordelia Cardigan stood flushed with embarrassment and cheap publisher's wine.

'I am now told,' said DJ, scratching his head thoughtfully, 'this Seth Sahib is being no good. He has made undue profit from my poem. And I am thinking to myself and saying, does it really matter in this life whether I am considered the writer of those words or Seth Sahib is? The important thing is that the voice of our people is being heard in the four corners of the world. And that, good people gathered here today, is all that matters, no?'

What a fine speech it was, full of courage and conviction. After hearing it, my own quest for justice and revenge seemed curiously futile and irrelevant. With a few simple words, D. J. Burman had shown true nobility. On impulse, I went up to the stage and embraced him in full emotional Bombay *filmi* style.

'You are right, brother. What matters is the voice, not the throat from which it sings.'

Sounds of 'Bravo, Bravo' were filling the air when suddenly Seth's Oxford accent cut through the hum of approval.

'Ladies and gentlemen, before applauding or taking sides, I beg you to consider this individual standing in front of you. Behaving in his typically theatrical, maudlin way is a specimen of what a poet should *not* be. Let me introduce Kavi Naidu, yes, him with the over-emotional crocodile tears running down his over-fed cheeks. Kavi Naidu claims to be a poet' – here Seth tried to mimic my voice – '"in the tradition of Shakespeare and Tennyson". I entreat you all to judge for yourself. Recite, Naidu, recite as only you can.'

Spurred on by this vicious attack, Seth grabbed a wine bottle and took quick, greedy gulps.

Given such an unexpected, below-the-belt introduction, it was not surprising that I fumbled. With one masterstroke, Seth the consummate operator had deflected the spotlight from D. J. Burman on to me. Without a manuscript nearby, verses became mixed in my mind. I talked about love, then grew confused as snatches from another, much older, poem about the beauty of old age came to mind.

'Sunset and evening star,
And one clear call for me.
And may there be no moaning of the bar
When I put out to sea.'

No sooner was this last line said than my memory played tricks on me again and the very first poem I had

216

written on Kamala's wifely loyalty broke out from my lips.

> 'Let me tonight of love
> To you speak.
> Just as the silvery strands of ageing hair
> Echo the moon,
> So the hands of this clock will one day
> Steal away our youth.
> And. . .'

In desperation, I seized on the fragment of another poem.

> 'There is sweet music here
> That softer falls
> Than petals from blown roses
> On the grass.'

Confused, I stopped mid-stanza and looked around for assistance. A growing crowd had gathered around me, the most visible member being Mrs Watanabe, who was swaying from side to side, solid arms folded against her chest, head nodding, large, wholesome tears flowing down her cheeks in utter disregard for convention.

'You can't have finished, surely? Go on, you're doing a fantastic job.' It was the gentleman in the blue blazer, speaking in a loud American-accented voice.

Frantically I continued, now beyond thinking.

> 'The smell of incense in the evening air,
> A mother's hand massaging your hair,
> A child gazing lovingly into your eyes,

While your wife waits, trembling with sighs.
Can there be a truer heaven on earth?'

The American gentleman was the first to congratulate
me and ask for my phone number.

'That was great, you sure are in tune with your emotions. Hey, we need to talk. Now? Your place or mine?'
The barrage of questions he threw at me made me
dizzy.

The two spinsterish ladies, who were following him
like shadows, nodded eagerly in agreement. 'Real
untainted Utopian freshness,' said one, kindly offering
me a glass of wine. The impromptu recitation had left
me breathless and I was grateful for the drink.

'Yes, yes, there is a method to my madness.' I
laughed self-deprecatingly, stealing a sidelong glance
at Seth, who was listening to our conversational
exchange with ill-disguised envy.

'And how would you describe your particular type of
poetry?' a earnest voice floated up from the back.

I considered the question carefully. 'Well, there is *my*
style of writing, and then there is Mr Seth's.'

A dozen heads did an about-turn to look at the target
of my criticism. Seth, aware of the shift in support,
squirmed self-consciously, reaching for his cigarette
crutch with a scowl.

'I write like water from a gushing fountain, without
caring for form and style, while our illustrious friend
here directs his words through a hose-pipe, accurate
and to the point. Unless, of course, his inspiration
is borrowed from elsewhere.' Once again, I embraced
D. J. Burman in a show of poetic solidarity.

This witty allusion drew a loud giggle from Amma,

who was exchanging nods and smiles with the American gentleman.

'And who is the inspiration behind your word-juggling?' It was one of the spinster ladies again.

Wordlessly I could only point to my mother, who burst into tears at the unexpected tribute. Murmurs of 'How moving. Look at her in that lovely sari' passed among the audience, and Mrs Watanabe gallantly offered Amma her handkerchief.

Burman, who had listened carefully to this appreciation, put his arm around me.

'Yes, Naiduji is a natural performer. The words just come dancing out of his mouth. The future of Indian poetry is safe in his hands.'

That was all that was needed, a genuine statement of appreciation from a respected scholar; I was lifted to cloud nine.

It was clear that Cordelia Cardigan did not share these sentiments. She had listened to DJ's speech of forgiveness with a scowl gathering on her face, and my impromptu delivery only increased her annoyance.

'What a dimwit DJ's been! Weeks of planning ruined by his Gandhi act. You guys always botch up everything.'

'Live and let live, Miss Cardigan.' The wine running through my veins was making me feel warm and philosophical. 'Even Seth will face his karma one day. Just rejoice that there are people like D. J. Burman to lift the moral tone of this planet.'

*

The American gentleman was waiting for us outside the bookshop.

'Hi. My name's Doug Hyman, with an A. I found your poetry very interesting.'

'And which American publisher do you represent, Mr Hyman?' asked Amma, business-like, surveying him from top to toe.

'None at all. I'm with an American greetings-card company, Soothing Bells. Heard of it? And by the way, just call me Doug.'

Mr Doug snapped open a very smart briefcase, from which he retrieved a number of calling cards. He seemed surprised and disappointed that neither Amma nor I had heard of his company, and insisted on treating us to black coffee and blueberry muffins at a coffee shop with the fairy-tale name of Julie's Pantry.

'You see,' I explained apologetically, sipping my coffee, 'India being so distant from America, we still don't know much about your culture.'

'Okay.' Mr Doug seemed satisfied with my explanation. 'Well, Soothing Bells has an eighty per cent share of the US market and our turnover is triple our nearest rival's. Know what the company motto is?'

Without waiting for a polite negative, he stood up, hand on heart, and in solemn style recited the following lines:

> 'From Cradle to Grave,
> Make no mistake,
> We shall be there
> Holding your hand.
> No occasion too big,
> No occasion too small.
> Just send your loved ones a
> Soothing Bells card.'

'Why, that's just like one of Naidu's poems!' Amma squealed in delight. 'I mean, you heard him tonight.'

'I know.' Mr Doug nodded, equally excited. 'Why else do you think I'm talking to you? I wondered if Mr Naidu could pen us a few words regularly – you know, sensitive stuff for things like Yom Kippur or Thanksgiving. We're always looking for a fresh angle on things. Isn't it wonderful I just happened to stroll into that bookshop at the right time?'

He beamed at us. He had unbuttoned his blazer, and looked quite boyish with his flushed red cheeks, his sand-coloured hair riding his forehead like a wave.

While Amma and Mr Doug discussed the practicalities involved in such an arrangement, I pondered the events of the evening. Although everything had gone in my favour, one slight detail niggled. In my haste to declaim my poetry, I had inadvertently quoted lines from Tennyson as my own.

'Isn't that a bit like Seth?' I asked Amma.

But Amma was quick to reassure me that this mingling of styles was what poetic liberty was about.

As far as Soothing Bells was concerned, I must say the idea appealed to me. Loud and eager as Mr Doug was, he represented a noble industry. Out there in America, caught in the money-making rat race, were tired, lonely souls desperate for the right words to build a bridge. What could be nobler than helping them, in my own modest way, to communicate and express their emotions? Surely this was poetry for the public good? Rather than accumulating trophies and medals for my own selfish glory, I would in this way be helping the ordinary, harassed citizens of America bond closer together.

'I agree wholeheartedly, Mr Doug, whatever the terms and conditions.' I leaned forward and impulsively clasped his hand, while beside me Amma shifted in her seat and kicked my ankle under the table.

*

It was late by the time we got back to the hotel. The lobby lay drowned in black, and in our room we discovered that Amma's bed had mysteriously disappeared. We had no choice but to wake Mrs Pereira.

My repeated knocking failed to rouse her and I was just reconciling myself to spending the night on the floor when a sliver of light under Matthew Joseph's door caught my eye.

It was with a heavy, all-knowing heart that I pushed open the door. It was like reliving that night in Manchester with Father O'Brian or that long-ago afternoon with Sharmila Sharma. And it was just as I'd suspected. Matthew Joseph lay naked on the bed, arms and legs outspread, a saint ready for sacrifice. Sitting on him, like a triumphant Goddess Kali, was Mrs Pereira, pink nightie pulled right up over her face, mother-of-pearl cross swinging dreamily between her shiny, dark, still-young breasts.

Even then the drama of the day had not yet ended, for soon afterwards my sleep was broken by a long-distance call from India. An angry Mrs Pereira, shameless Matthew Joseph in tow, banged loudly on the door.

'Please, I will not be having this any more. Day and night, your relatives keep harassing twenty-four hours. This is a hard-working hotel, we all have to sweat overtime for our sleep-time here.'

A sobbing Feroze came on the line. He refused to

speak to me, crying instead for Amma. '*Dadi.* I want *Dadi,* not you,' he kept repeating dully.

Impatiently Amma snatched the phone. But instead of Feroze, it was Mrs Basu she spoke to. Something was wrong, desperately wrong, for Amma's face went a sickly *chappati* colour. After a series of abrupt, shouted whens and wheres she replaced the receiver quietly and requested a glass of brandy.

'But, Amma, you never drink. What is it? Feroze? Has he had an accident? Failed his exams?'

The urgency in my voice finally penetrated.

'It is that insufferable woman Mrs Basu again. Just who does she think she is, the *Hindustan Times*? The exclusive purveyor and surveyor of all the evil news in the world.'

'Well, what did she say?' I was getting frantic.

'Something black in the lentil soup,' Amma muttered ominously. 'It is our Kamala. She has flown the nest.'

CHAPTER TWENTY-EIGHT

An abrupt homecoming

The rhyming, chiming tick-tock of time
The perfume of forgotten roses.
The smiles of forgotten faces.
Half-felt shadows and suns
Leaving their tender mark upon the skin.
Naidu reluctantly comes of age.

(Inaugural poem published in the *Illustrated Weekly Views*)

'LISTENJI, THE WATER has boiled for your bath.' Like all good Indian wives, Kamala seldom addressed me by my name, preferring the formality of the third person.

'Listenji, the *paratha* is piping hot, your favourite *gobi* one. Leave your newspaper and eat it fast, please.'

These Listenjis summed up much of our married life. Unending requests for me to try the ironed trousers, taste the first mango pickle of the season, allow my legs to be massaged after a hard day's work.

And me? What had I offered her in return? Constant rebukes and criticisms. 'Kamala, you know I prefer omelette not *paratha* for breakfast. Must you teach Feroze Hindi nursery rhymes? What's the point of sending him to an English-medium school?'

And always Kamala listening to me in stubborn silence, eyes fixed on my shoes, drawing her *sari-pallu* a little tighter round her shoulders, which stooped a little more with each passing year. One day the thread must simply have snapped. Somewhere on her daily trip between home and temple, Kamala had decided to break free.

Hadn't Father warned us of this? 'Stop behaving like Christian crusaders, you two. Let her be or one day, you'll see, there will be no bed-tea, just all-round regrets.'

With these thoughts pounding through my head, I prepared for the return home.

'You think time grows on trees?' With these fond words of farewell, Mrs Pereira prepared to bundle us off to Heathrow in a waiting taxi.

She was right. The Air India flight was leaving in two hours, but so numb was I with the news of Kamala's disappearance that even the simple act of packing had been heavy with loss and betrayal. Amma, showing her characteristic pragmatic streak, had left me in charge of it, while she went post-haste with Gonzales to a nearby Woolworth's store, Feroze's wretched shopping list held firmly in her hand.

There were some final goodbyes that needed to be made. Quietly I dialled Mr Mistry's number. He had done so much for me; it was only right that I should pay my last respects. With Naina I had no wish to reopen any dialogue, although in view of the recent happenings I made allowances for her behaviour. After all, if a simple housewife and mother from Delhi could shrug off her duties and obligations in a moment, what right had I to expect virtuous behaviour from a woman of such seasoned sophistication as Naina?

Mr Mistry's cultured voice answered the phone. 'My dear Naidu, how distraught and jumbled together you sound. I hope nothing is amiss?' He listened sympathetically to my news and regretted the unexpectedly early departure. 'What a shame, and just when we had decided to read your poems. But I suppose you must leave. A wife cannot simply disappear into thin air like that. Most inconsiderate of her.'

I laughed weakly at his wit.

He seemed in unusually high spirits. 'As a matter of fact, Naina mentioned you only this morning. You remember O'Brian? Well, he is opening an alternative medical centre specialising in herbal treatments, just off the coast of Ireland, and she was wondering if you could join her there. A most refreshing part of the world, all that clean fresh air and pints of Guinness. Pity you will miss all that, Naidu. Oh, here she is. You can say your goodbyes yourself.'

Naina was all sweetness and light. 'So the homing pigeon flies home at last. Such a shame about the poetry. Mind you, it is never too late to make a fresh start. Ever considered accountancy?'

A lump rose in my throat. When all was said and done, the Mistrys had played a significant role in my English sojourn, and Naina, despite her promiscuous ways, was, after all, responsible for introducing me to my own manhood.

There was one other farewell call I had to make.

'But you can't be leaving now, not when your cock is

crowing so loudly!' An excited Mrs Watanabe refused to believe I was leaving England so soon. 'Goodbyes cannot be whispered on the phone. I am coming in person to fill you up with my blessings.'

She appeared what seemed only moments later, while Amma and I were stuffing Feroze's chocolates and comics into the reluctant mouth of the Aeroflot bag.

'Mother, cherish your son, he will be the Poet for Tomorrow.'

Amma, intent on redoing my packing, gave a careless nod at Mrs Watanabe's maternal advice. Persuaded at last that my fellow poet could not pose a romantic threat, she allowed us to say our farewells in the lobby.

Tapping my chest twice, Mrs Watanabe coyly moved my hand down her frilly, low-necked dress. 'There, give them an old-fashioned goodbye squeeze. As we say in Tonga, "A healthy heart and a hearty cock make even the poor man fit for the Queen." Look after them both, my friend.'

Moved by this parting speech, she left in a flood of tears, waving her Peking fan in a last gesture of farewell.

*

The hot, sullen Delhi air greeted us like a slap. The Basus were standing there, just behind Customs, grimly triumphant we-knew-it-all-along expressions on their faces. Dust lay everywhere: on the trees, on the people. London, with its clean, pure-cut lines, suddenly seemed a lifetime away.

Strawberries and cream.
Endless cups of Twinings tea.

227

Old ladies with poodles trotting home.
How I will miss
The beauty of an English summer's noon.

'Same old Delhi,' I said to Amma with a sigh as Mr Basu clumsily manoeuvred his Fiat Padmini around a pond-sized pothole on the Ring Road.

'You are sounding proper foreign-returned now,' Mrs Basu said admiringly, forcing a sticky, limp *rosgulla* into my mouth. 'Just like our Mrs Gandhi with her Italian daughter-in-law.'

*

'There was something fishy all along,' said Mrs Basu self-righteously. 'Being a Bengali, I could smell that. But tell me, *behanji*, what could I say? After all, a *bahu* was concerned. How can one point fingers at another's private affairs? And you being such a busy political lady with your Nehru meetings and all. You must thank your stars that I am your eyes and ears on the road.' She pushed another plate of *sandesh* towards Amma. 'Here, have some more tits and bits.'

The Kamala post-mortem was being conducted in Mrs Basu's drawing room. Framed certificates of her son's academic achievements crowed from every wall. An imported fridge and television set (the Basus had close relatives in Singapore), covered carefully with a lace tablecloth, occupied pride of place, next to a gar-landed portrait of Mr Basu's late father.

'What do you mean, Mrs Basu? Explain yourself.' There was an edge to Amma's voice.

'Come on, *behanji*. You of all the people should know. It all started with the opening of that Krishna Centre.

228

Those hippies! They polluted the whole neighbourhood. Things were never the same again.'

Mrs Basu stopped and looked at Feroze, who sat, tearfully sucking his knee, on the edge of an imported Chinese armchair. 'Feroze, *beta*, would you like to play some carom-board or read some *Archie* comics? Run along to Chintu Uncle's room, now.

'The point is' – she was warming to her theme – 'ever since that Centre opened, Kamala *beti* has not been herself. You remember those hippies distributing those pamphlet-vamphlets around the houses?'

I shook my head.

'No, no, not you, *beta*. How would you know anything, with your head swimming in poetic clouds?' She turned again to Amma. 'Fancy those Americans trying to teach us about Lord Krishna. Stainless steel to Sheffield, I say.

'These same pamphlets Kamala would take to Panditji at the Hanuman temple and pester him with questions about, you know . . .' Mrs Basu paused, trying to remember. 'Yes, big issues like Nirvana and the soul. Panditji was most angry, he told me so himself when I went there to make friendly enquiries. Filling her head overnight with all these big American ideas, when all Kamala really had to do was make sure the temple steps were clean and that enough women turned up punctually for the evening *darshan*. Yes, the trouble started then. In fact, just a few days after your son left for England.'

Mrs Basu waited for our reaction. When no suitable response was forthcoming, her hand disappeared inside her blouse, from where she fished out a creased envelope.

'This is for you, *beta*,' she said, handing it to me.

'But it has been opened?' I looked at her accusingly.

'Of course it is open. I had to read it first, for the common good. It was left under the Ganesha statue in your room.' And she pushed a plate of freshly fried *alu tikkis* towards us.

The letter, written in broken English, was from Kamala.

Dear husband, lord and master,
You must be shocked, being in England and your wife running away from the safe roof under which you covered her head so many years. But I could not help myself. Prabhu Das (John Stern, from Wisconsin, America) opened my eyes to real Kamala.

Yes, my lord and master, I am leaving you and dear Feroze who is a piece of my heart. Hare Krishna temple and Prabhu Das is my future now. They will show me the right path to myself now. Please ask Amma to forgive her sin-filled bahu and remember me in your English poems.

Silently I passed the letter to Amma. Despite the atrocious grammar, I found it quite moving and to the point. Kamala's soul had no doubt been corrupted by this crooked Prabhu Das, but then who was I to throw the first stone, fresh as I was from my English sinning?

It was Amma who spoke first. 'You know, this letter has lifted a heavy burden from my shoulders, Mrs Basu.'

I looked at her, puzzled. Indeed the light had re-entered Amma's eyes, and her face looked relaxed again.

'You see,' she explained, 'I was afraid that Kamala was chasing her tiresome gods again, had become a *sanyasin* or something, and that would mean both Naidu and I had failed – thirteen years in an enlightened household gone for nothing. But this is different.' A broad smile covered her face. 'Kamala is chasing herself, not some clay shadow. She has discovered the individual. I am sure Nehruji would have said the same.'

Mrs Basu looked devastated by this interpretation of events. She had clearly been expecting us to dissolve into a *Mahabharata* of tears and lamentations.

'No, *behanji*, this time you can't hide behind clever big words. The truth is your daughter-in-law has brought shame to your name, running away with a *gora*. The whole neighbourhood is buzzing alive with rumours. It will be most difficult for you to hold your head high again. I am sure Mr Basu will be more than willing to help you to relocate, perhaps to some small town in UP like Bareily or Bikaner.'

'Mrs Basu, are you chasing us out of our own house? Like jackals you think we should slink away, our tails tucked within our legs? Absolutely not.'

'So you will be pressing no charges, filing no complaints, against this notorious Kamala?' Tears of disappointment threatened to flood Mrs Basu's eyes.

Amma shook her head emphatically and, catching hold of Feroze, who had reappeared with a bundle of comics under his arm, indicated that the inquest was over.

Later that night, when Feroze was asleep, I removed the borrowed comics from under his pillow. Lurking between the bumper issues of *Batman* and *Casper* was the very same German magazine that had tantalised my flesh in those long-ago afternoons of my childhood. Sadly, I looked at my son's sleeping twelve-year-old face. How history never tired of repeating itself.

In the privacy of my room, I leafed through the magazine and the images it contained. This time there was no racing of pulse, no boiling of blood. Directly or indirectly I had experienced at first hand all the perversions and imaginative twists the magazine could offer. Naidu had most definitely come of age.

I slept badly that night, and the old dream about the *Ben-Hur* film set returned, only this time the Caesar munching grapes and figs was me, not Mistry, and the adoring *Apsaras* were two buxom Germanic girls with heavy blond plaits and cherry-red mouths.

The next day, I decided to investigate the Hare Krishna Centre. Stepping cautiously past the acres of washing spread out to dry in the *dhobi* colony, I stopped to admire the architecture of the temple. The marble steps were scrupulously clean and large flowerbeds of blazing yellow dahlias highlighted the whiteness of the walls.

One Jai Dev, a slim Englishman wearing a pale orange dhoti, met me at the door. The main prayers had just finished and the gods sat dozing behind heavy velvet curtains. A strong smell of incense and fried puris lingered in the air, and in the far corner of the main hall a small group of English children, shaven-headed and dressed in dhotis, were being quietly taught by a red-haired lady in a sari.

'I must say, this is most impressive,' I complimented Jai Dev. 'So spick and span. You should see the state of our temples.' I was thinking of our Hanuman temple, where one's bare feet were constantly curling against

232

rotting flower petals and spilled food, and the radio blared out shrill *bhajans* all day long.

He smiled politely, the ash smeared on his forehead trembling a little with emotion. 'Yes, we do things differently here. Since our opening not a single power-cut or water shortage has been reported.'

Jai Dev, I found out, had been an electrician in his previous incarnation and had lived in, of all places, Manchester.

'I have been there – a delightful place,' I lied.

'Delightful?' He raised his eyebrows. 'I was unemployed there for two years, the local council was pulling down our flat and then Dad ran off with a dinner lady. If this hadn't come along, I don't know where I'd be.'

His mouth shrank into a thin line as he said this, and I immediately regretted my cheerful remark.

On the question of Kamala's whereabouts, Jai Dev was not so forthcoming. Repeated questions met with the same determined shake of the head.

'How are we to know? The prayers we do attract so many locals. It's the free food the slum kids are after, especially the puris. Mind you, we do try to discourage the locals from attending regularly. Far too noisy and the kids leave too much dirt behind.' With these words, he briskly escorted me to the door. The Personal Enhancement class was starting soon, and devotees from their Canadian branch were expected any minute.

'Imperialist pigs, the lot of them!' Amma said angrily when I described the meeting. 'They come here, steal our gods and our sunshine, and then shut the door on us. I tell you, Kamala will soon see the light. She'll be back.'

I hoped deeply that she was right. Familiar Delhi felt coldly unfamiliar in the absence of Kamala. Where once I had ridiculed the simple pitter-patter of her daily routine, I now found myself longing for its return. The Ganeshas in our room seemed inanimate and metallic in her absence, and Rouse Avenue wore an abandoned air. In a house, a city, devoid of Kamala, I was no longer sure of my place in the world. I felt lonelier now than I had ever done as a struggling outsider in England.

I have left the doors,
The windows, wide open,
Caught the sun-light,
Cupped the rain-drops,
In anticipation of
Your return one day.

CHAPTER TWENTY-NINE

Rouse Avenue, two years later

〜

TWO PECULIAR THINGS happened in Rouse Avenue the year Kamala disappeared.

The jamun tree suddenly, inexplicably, burst into fruit, and out of season too. For years it had stood in stubborn barrenness in the *maidan*, used as a cricketing stump by the local schoolboys. Then one day the moist round berries rained shamelessly to the ground, staining it a rich purple. Colourful ribbons began fluttering from every branch as the local women quickly transformed it into a shrine to fertility. Every Friday, the pandit from the nearby Hanuman temple held special prayer sessions for childless women in the shade of the tree.

The second strange thing was the disappearance of Amma's beloved goat. Feroze came running into the house one morning, school satchel banging against pencil-thin brown legs, voice shrill in excitement. 'Billy-goat is gone! Run away!' He was right. It had vanished, just like that, into the thick, hot Delhi smog.

Dear Naidu,
It is rarely that old students fulfil the promise of their early

years. But the sensitivity and maturity you have shown in handling a subject as difficult as the status of mothers in modern India, convinces me that I have not failed as a teacher.

*

It was also at Billo's that I resumed my friendship with my old friends Sharmila Sharma and Binoy. We met on the last Saturday of every month, a sort of writers' club where we talked about the good old days and our mutual friends, all thankfully now settled in respectable professions. Sharmila herself had long since broken off her bohemian associations and settled into married respectability with a rich Marwari businessman who exported spectacle frames to the Gulf. Considerably plumper now, and dressed always in soft chiffon saris and diamond ear studs, she was the proud mother of two Doon School-attending sons.

'Life,' Sharmila gravely informed me at one of these meetings, 'does a funny somersault and throws you right back where you started. Take you, for instance. Weren't you supposed to shake the English-speaking world with your poems? And what is the highlight of your weekly diary now? Ramming rhyming couplets down the throats of reluctant housewives.'

'No, Sharmila, no,' I contradicted her, as she snapped open her foreign bag to extract yet another box of imported chocolates, the wrappers of which (each showing a slice of Swiss landscape) would be absent-mindedly scattered on the floor. Since her affluent marriage, she had acquired a distaste of all things *desi* and homegrown. Gone were the crisp cottons of her youth; she now favoured imported Japanese chiffon from Hong Kong. Even her drinking water, she

236

boasted, came all the way from Milan, the product of an Italian joint venture.

Sharmila's insistence on viewing my life as some kind of anti-climax irritated me no end. For some reason, she refused to believe that my childish hankering after fame and glory had been replaced by inner harmony and peace. It was Burman who had shown me the way, by refusing to be drawn into a tug-of-war with Seth. True, I had shrunk the boundaries of my world, but at least it was one in which I could walk with my head held high.

How could I expect Sharmila, with her kitty-card sessions, her shopping trips to Singapore, her *nautch*-girl parties at Diwali, to understand that? How different she had become from the *bidi*-smoking, silver-bangled, Lenin-quoting girl writing in a one-roomed *barsati*.

It was around this time that I went to the British Council, to fulfil a boyhood dream. A signed first edition of *Hamlet Through an Eastern Eye*, a monograph I had recently completed, was being donated to the library.

The reading room seemed a bit faded now. The marble, worn and yellow, needed a polish and the bookshelves teetered precariously beneath their load. Even the Anglo-Indian librarians were like shadows, the celebrated pink of their cheeks turned to a sickly yellow. I sat on one of the sagging sofas and idly flicked through the newspapers while they fluttered about me, helplessly wringing their hands. It was then that I saw it: the matter-of-fact announcement, on the second page of a month-old *Times*, of the initiation of divorce proceedings between Mr Mistry, the Indian High Commissioner to London, and his wife.

I immediately rang up Binoy, who had abandoned his ponytail and worked for a respectable American newsagency, the Voice of America. The Mistrys, Binoy informed me, had separated soon after Mr Mistry's involvement with a Russian ballet dancer from the Bolshoi became public knowledge. He was now cultivating olives with her in some beautiful part of Italy.

'And Naina?' Even after so long, the sound of her name could cause an anxious skip in my heartbeat.

'Oh, the wife? Quite a fast one, wasn't she? Real hot stuff, eh?' Binoy's voice was sly with innuendo. But I refused to give in to his indelicate probing. Defiling a woman's reputation was not in my character.

It took me a month before I could ascertain her whereabouts from an absent-minded Binoy.

'That woman again? Naidu, I'm sure there was some hanky-panky between the two of you. Didn't I tell you? She's moved to some place in America – California, I think. Apparently, they practise "Free Love" there.' Binoy giggled like a teenager at the words.

CHAPTER THIRTY

Some endings, some beginnings

~

AMMA WAS NEVER the same after our return from England. A strange restlessness settled over her, and she began to find the little rituals of daily life in Rouse Avenue irritating. The dahlias in pots on the veranda, which she had once watered so lovingly, quietly shrivelled, unattended, a fine film of spider's web forming over their leaves. Impatiently, she wandered from room to room, the beloved Murphy transistor tucked under her arm.

'There is no backbone to the day here, Naidu, too much sitting around and drinking cups of tea.'

'But, Amma, you've only just returned. Now is the time to sit back, relax and take things easy. How about writing a memoir about your experiences running the Nehru Society?'

'Nonsense! Who would listen to the ranting of an ancient woman? Everybody is only interested in money these days. No, Naidu, my time is up. I can feel the blood slowing down. As for you, look, it's already midday and you still haven't had a bath. In your place, by this time I'd have finished two rounds of lectures at the University, attended a poetry-appreciation class and given an interview to Mark Tully for the BBC.'

Strange as it sounded, and although the excursion had been but brief, Amma was missing England. Back in Rouse Avenue, with no Kamala to chastise and mould, no eager intrigue to further my poetic career, life felt, in her words, 'as dull as a flat soufflé'. I did my best to distract her, suggesting picnics in the Lodhi Gardens, with her favourite cold coffee in a thermos flask, or a visit to Kanpur, where her elder brother held a franchise for Charminar cigarettes. But with a brusque 'Frivolous pursuits, not meant for me,' she rejected every offer of entertainment. More worryingly, I, who had once occupied such a central role in her life, now shrank into the same category of insignificant endeavours.

In a comment that chillingly reminded me of Seth's, she turned to me one day, fixed me with an all-appraising stare, and said, 'It is entirely my fault that you have remained infantile for so long, Naidu. No wonder your poetry is missing that sweaty smell of real life. High time you rolled up your sleeves and did a decent day's work. All this business of sunsets and fountains drying in grief is utter paper-wasting bull-shit!' Yes, she sounded just like Seth.

Not content with words, Amma set about transforming Rouse Avenue into a mini replica of a Russian gulag. I came home one day to find that our beds had been donated to the Upliftment of Washerwomen charity. Threadbare *dhurris*, purchased at cost price from the Khadi emporium in Connaught Place, were thrown on the floor instead. Slowly but steadily, the other minor comforts of life began trickling out of the house. The toaster was soon followed by the television and the once-cherished Hitkari tea set.

'We go around with too much excess baggage' was Amma's justification for every item that went missing.

Word soon spread about her unusual largesse, and every morning misfits from all four corners of Delhi congregated hopefully outside our house, staking their claim on yet another domestic possession. The final straw was when Amma handed over her prized PhD thesis to a sinister-looking junkyard dealer from Faridabad with betel nut-stained teeth.

This eccentric behaviour, at first endearing, had become downright annoying.

'Amma, please stop this nonsense. It is not 1947 any more. This is our home, not the headquarters of some civil disobedience movement.'

She listened quietly, refusing to offer a single word in her defence, merely shaking her head from time to time.

Munimji, who was visiting at the time, tactfully took me aside. 'Gentle approach works best with the old. Your mother most definitely has gone senile after her foreign trip. Look at me now, eighty years of age and still taking England in my stride.'

The air that morning hung smoky and crisp. Dusshera had just ended and the giant burned effigies of Ravan and his two brothers lay sulking in various parts of the city, releasing slow, charred ashes into the air. The sweepers were late starting their work and the road was littered with discarded sweet boxes and the blackened shells of firework crackers.

'Just look at all this filth,' Amma said crossly before calling Mundu to start sweeping the front. 'You should have seen the daily rubdown Mrs Pereira gave her hotel. Spotless and A1 everything was. That is what this country needs, a Mrs Pereira's hand.'

I smiled indulgently at Amma's outburst before settling down to work. Mr Doug wanted me to write a set of poems commemorating the American festival of Thanksgiving. These poems, with their theme of family ties and love of the land, were close to my heart. Words burst from me spontaneously, singing from my pen. One poem went like this:

Family ties that bind
With love and tears
Through the years.
This Thanksgiving Day
Come, let us rejoice and unite.

From time to time I consulted the American map, in order to refresh my memory about the 'swaying corn-fields of Iowa', or the 'sunshine that drips like honey' in the state of Florida. So immersed was I in my word-crafting that at first I didn't hear Mundu's frantic screaming. It was only when he rushed into my room, eyes saucer-wide in fear, whimpering, 'Ammaji, Ammaji,' that I knew something was dreadfully amiss.

Amma sat awkwardly, slumped almost out of her chair. The wispy *pallu* of her sari had fallen forward, covering the transistor radio like a shroud. An inter-view with Lord Mountbatten was blaring into the smoky sunshine. The interviewer's cool, crisp BBC voice was asking whether he still missed his wife, Edwina, after all these years.

For some reason, Mountbatten's reply seemed critical to the shaping of that morning. 'You know, missing someone is one of those infinite, interminable things. You can't put a date to it and say it has to stop now.'

I looked at Amma. A fly hovered cautiously over the saliva drying in one corner of her slightly parted lips. Her eyes, wide open, seemed annoyed, as though death had sneaked up on her from behind and taken her by surprise. I shook her, gently at first and then roughly, angry with her for not replying. For not preparing me for this sudden departure.

*

News of Amma's passing spread rapidly through Rouse Avenue. By early afternoon a sympathetic crowd had collected on the sheet-covered veranda. The buttery pandit, whom Amma had loathed vehemently in her lifetime, arrived uninvited, armed with the appropriate paraphernalia for mourning the dead: incense sticks, marigolds and a rusty, shrill tape of plaintive hymns.

Since her return from England, Amma had become revered in the neighbourhood as a kind of heroic modern-day Durga, principled and strong, who had managed to win back her son from the temptations of the West. A few ladies had even named their baby daughters after her. They were all assembled here today, eyes lowered, hands folded, filing past a girlish black-and-white photo of her which I had dug out from the Nehru Society archives. Leading the mourning was Munimji, who in startling non-anglicised behaviour, loudly berated the passing of a 'fine upstanding lady'.

Somehow the day passed. Mrs Basu, all old animosities forgotten, had purposefully taken charge of the household. The kitchen was shut down and Feroze dispatched to her relatives in Chitteranjan Park. Amma's body, draped in the Indian tricolour and the Union Jack, was to be whisked away to the Lodi Ghat crematorium. Her face, washed clean of all expression, stared back at me peacefully from the taxi seat where Munimji sat cradling her head on his lap. Dressed again in his three-piece suit, he seemed in control of his emotions.

'Most absolutely not', he said vehemently, brushing aside my every entreaty to accompany Amma's body to the crematorium. 'Not for anything in the world would your mother have wanted your delicate, poetic soul exposed to such a sight. Worry not, *beta*, she will be given a fitting farewell. Her work will continue. The Nehru Society will be renamed the Shobha Naidu Society for Social Advancement.'

I listened silently, grateful for the words of reassurance.

Slowly the house emptied of visitors, and, as night fell, unfamiliar shadows seemed to collect in little pools of darkness around the rooms. After so many years, I was about to spend a night alone in Rouse Avenue, without the sound of Amma's breathing in the next room.

> *The umbrella has been snatched away from me,*
> *The umbrella of a mother's love.*
> *Who will now shelter me from the sun and rain*
> *Of the passing years?*

Unable to continue, I went out on the veranda. The air was thick with the smell of cow dung being burned in the washerwomen's *bustee* as preparations for the evening meal commenced. Little heaps of ash from burned-out incense sticks brushed against my bare feet.

There was a sudden footfall on the outside step. Switching on the light, I stirred a cloud of sleeping insects back to life. Framed against the pale yellow light of the bulb stood Kamala. Dressed in a soft silk sari, a small bundle tucked under her arm, she stood before me, holding me with that same dark expressionless gaze. The plumpness of her rounded shoulders had gone, as had the shadow of a double chin. Her hair, normally well-oiled and plaited, lay loose and free upon those shoulders. Two damp patches of sweat clung to the inside of her arms. The sight excited me. Ashamed, I looked away.

Without saying a single word she bent down to touch my feet. Abashed, I raised her quickly and tried once more to read the darkness within her eyes.

'Why have you chosen to return now?' I asked.

'Because you have chosen to need me now,' she whispered.

*

Waking later that night from a restless sleep, I became aware of Kamala lying next to me. Her face, heavy with sleep, looked almost peaceful by the light of the moon filtering through the shutters. Quietly, I traced the centre parting of her hair, which still smelled of Shikkai soap, and removed the red *bindi* still adorning her forehead, revealing a tiny crease of worry. My eyes travelled down to where the dark shadows gathered under the curve of her breasts. Gently I gathered them, turning her towards me. Kamala's eyes flew open, like two startled birds shaken awake, and a slow smile softly tiptoed into them.

245

All BlackAmber Books are available from your local bookshop.

For a regular update on BlackAmber's latest release, with extracts, reviews and events, visit:

www.blackamber.com